Charmed by Chocolate

Charmed by Chocolate

A Love at the Chocolate Shop Romance

Steena Holmes

TULE
PUBLISHING

Chapter One

"I CAME HOME why again?" The view outside her front window did nothing to convince Leah coming back had been a good idea.

She'd exchanged green grass, rolling hills, and soft sea breezes for freezing snow, flat land, and chilling blizzard winds.

If she had to do it all over again, coming back here should have been the last option.

Who was she kidding? This had been her only option.

She ran home to lick her wounds and this…this cold, never-ending white stuff outside was the price to pay.

One freakish blizzard after the other. Almost as if Mother Nature herself was trying to keep Leah in Marietta.

A chilly burst of air from the crack at the bottom of the front door wound its way around her ankles and nipped at her skin. Her four pairs of wool socks were sitting in the washing machine along with her only comfy pair of Mukluks. Thanks to Dylan's cat, Jack, all she had left were ankle socks. Who wore ankle socks during the winter in Montana?

Dang cat and his miserable temperament.

She'd been home for exactly twenty-four hours, but she'd forgotten how cold Marietta could get in the winter. She'd expected all her winter gear would still be here, but her brother gave it all away during a clothing drive last year.

Nice one, Dylan.

When she'd said she'd never return to Marietta, he'd apparently believed her.

He should know her better than that. She might say words she regretted in the heat of the moment…but that was all they were…words.

As if she could get Marietta out of her system.

She didn't mind coming back to visit…but she preferred coming back in the summer—when it was sweltering hot.

Her favorite time to come back was during the rodeo. Not in March.

Southern California never got this cold. Ever.

Leah shivered and drew the ends of her cardigan closer to her small-framed body.

"Is today the day I'm going to face the world?" Leah tossed the question over to Jack, who laid on his bed in front of the floor heater, ignoring her.

"That's what I thought. Licking my wounds a little while longer it is." Leah went to lightly rub the cat's head, but his deep growl had her pulling away. There were enough scratch marks on her hands to know he was an ornery old thing.

"One day, you'll like me. I don't care if it takes all the

time in the world, either."

She eyed the heavily blanketed sidewalk in front of the house and knew she needed to go out and clean it off before anyone from the retirement home down the street went for their daily walk. Dylan sent a message earlier saying he'd take care of it when he got home, but if she bundled up, no one would recognize her. Right?

Whether it was the cold draft snaking around her ankles or just watching the snow fall, goose bumps started to cover her body and Leah shivered. She'd turned the kettle on earlier for tea. Hopefully, it was still hot. She'd prefer hot chocolate, but after convincing Dylan to bring home a carafe of Sage's delectable concoction last night, she'd never go back to the pre-packaged garbage her brother kept in the cupboard.

Leah reached for the tattered brown-and-blue knitted scarf Wade had made for her one Christmas, wrapping its softness around her neck before pouring boiling water into an awaiting mug of tea. The moment she wrapped her hands around the hot mug, she sighed with relief, enjoying the warmth as it seeped into her palms. Now, if only her fingers would de-ice.

Of all the places in this home she missed the most, it was this kitchen. So many sweet memories of her life had started here. Baking with her mother as a little girl, learning how to read recipes, create treats from scratch…she cherished those moments. Her mom would tell her stories about her past, of growing up and learning how to bake herself. She shared stories about how her and Leah's father met, fell in love, and then stories about her and her brother, and then all those memories where her mother gave her advice about her friendships, her failed relationships, and then with…

No. Leah clamped down on all thoughts about that…stuff.

It made her miss her parents even more. They'd been gone for over fifteen years now, having died in a tragic car accident where they were forced off the road by a truck full of drunken teens.

Losing her parents at the age of eighteen had changed her life in more ways than one.

Leah dedicated her life to working with teens, speaking at assemblies, and even volunteered as a designated driver on the weekends…anything to do her part in making sure they were aware of the dangers of drinking and driving. Saving lives was her focus and goal.

She hoped she hadn't screwed that up by her latest faux pas.

Leah picked at one of the fresh-baked chocolate chip oatmeal muffins she'd made earlier this morning. The plate of cinnamon buns she'd made in the middle of the night after not being able to sleep called out to her, but she'd save those as a reward for shoveling.

Food made for great rewards.

"Sorry about the blizzard, folks. Apparently, March is

coming in like a lion this year and not the lamb I'd predicted." Dylan, her brother as well as Marietta's local radio DJ
and weatherman's voice, caught her attention on the radio
she had playing in the background. "Keep those ice skates
handy, though, as the weather should break by midafter-
noon. And remember, I may not always get the weather
right, but I can make your mood better thanks to the sounds
of our next music artist, Garth Brooks."

Leah snickered at the apologetic tone to his voice. She
could imagine the phone calls her brother was getting at the
station. There was a running bet down at the local pub
regarding Dylan and his weather guarantees.

Leah took a sip of her tea and enjoyed the scorching sen-
sation as she swallowed.

By the time she was bundled up with her brother's oversized hooded jacket, waterproof mitts, knitted hat, and his
extra-large snow boots, she was sweating.

The street outside was quiet. The falling snow muted the
sounds of traffic down the street. For a moment...a very
brief moment...Leah relished the stillness. Until cold
puddles of liquid soaked through the bottoms of the discarded boots she'd found in the front closet.

Now she knew why they'd been buried at the back of the
closet.

Leah bit back a groan, pulled up the scarf around her
neck to cover her mouth and nose, reached for the shovel
that rested just inside the small alcove of the front porch, and

started the arduous process of clearing away the fluffy, yet dense snow.

She hated winter. Hated it with a passion. Every year since moving away, she'd send Dylan photos of her enjoying the warm sun whenever she checked the weather and saw it'd snowed in Marietta. Every photo she sent, Dylan would reply with a warning that karma had a nasty temperament. Of course, Leah ignored that.

Karma loved her. Karma would never turn on its heel and kick her in the butt. Karma was her best friend.

Until she did something to piss karma off.

Karma sucked.

With that in mind, Leah bent down and pushed her shovel along the sidewalk. When it was full, she lifted it up, aiming the snow to go flying over the curb and onto the road in front of her. Except a gust of wind hit her and carried the snow behind her. A muffled gasp caught her attention. Leah spun, her eyes widening in dismay as her grandmother wiped snow off her face.

"Oh my…Grams! I'm so sorry." She dropped the shovel. "I didn't realize you were behind me, and the wind—" Leah rushed over and brushed snow off her grandmother's coat and scarf.

Grams brushed her hands away, relinquished her hold of the man's arm beside her, and smoothed her bright red winter coat. "I always did like a good snowball fight." Her eyes twinkled while the color in her cheeks matched her coat.

"Wade, be a dear and finish clearing Leah's sidewalk?"

Leah froze. Her mouth flapped like a gasping fish.

"Close your mouth, Leah, it's unbecoming." Grams tapped her on the sleeve.

Leah's hand tightened around the shovel but did as she was told, like a little child.

Wade Burns. Damn the man. Karma must really have it out for her right now.

"I'm not ready for you. Not yet." The words made their way out of her mouth before she even knew she thought them.

The way his eyes softened at her words made her want to scream.

Not fair, Karma. Not fair.

Wade Burns was her best friend. Her soul mate. The one person she trusted more than anyone else in the world. Until last month, not a day went by when they weren't talking via text message, sharing a laugh on Facebook, or even messaging on Twitter. This was the one man who knew her inside and out, who loved her without prejudice. She treasured his friendship more than anything in the world, which was why seeing him here, now, when she wasn't ready…

Not fair, Karma. Not fair.

Exactly five days ago, she'd blurted out her love for him on national television.

It had been the five longest days of her life.

The five roughest days in the past few years.

Did he know? Was she living in a dream world by hoping he didn't?

Probably.

The nail that'd been hammered deep into her heart after that humiliating episode twisted, reopening the wound Wade himself had placed there, and she was surprised she was still standing.

She'd told him how she felt one night about a month ago, and he'd turned her down. Not just turned her down, though; he completely obliterated her by acting as if the words hadn't popped out of her mouth at all.

I love you.

Gah. She couldn't even look at him now.

"Well, kiddo," Grams nudged her out of the way, "ready or not, here I am." Her grandmother headed to the front door and climbed the steps. "Leah? Give the shovel to Wade."

Leah wordlessly handed the shovel over to the one man she'd hoped to avoid for a little while longer.

His soft, insanely gorgeous smile and wink confirmed he knew it, too.

"It's good to see you, Leah." His voice, the audible version of smooth butterscotch rum sliding down one's throat, had her weak in the knees. "I've been waiting for you to call or text…" He watched her with those kind, gorgeous eyes of his, and her heart started to tap-tap-tap against her chest. She rubbed at the spot, as if it actually ached, before dropping her hand, hoping he hadn't caught that little response.

"Something you need to get off your chest?" His low voice rumbled all the way through her.

"What? No...no...I just..." The words were all twisted up inside of her.

For Pete's sake, she was acting like a love-struck teenager, and there was nothing she could do about it.

"Child, get in the house." Grams' voice was full of laughter, leaving Leah wishing that dying from embarrassment was actually a real thing.

"Grams, you don't play fair," Leah hissed as she climbed the steps and opened the door, moving to the side so her grandmother could walk in first. She cast a quick glance down at Wade, who caught her looking and gave her one of those heart-thumping smiles of his.

The edges of her lips started to curl into something she hoped was a smile, but feared might actually look like a grimace. The sudden frown on his face confirmed that fear.

"I never have, love," Grams teased. Leah tore her gaze from Wade's and looked at her grandmother. "Why start playing fair now?" The saucy grin on Grams' face told Leah more than she needed to know.

She'd brought Wade here on purpose. Damn the woman.

"Do you have any salt or rock chips?" Wade asked before she could close the door.

Leah pointed to the round white container just off to the

side of the front porch. "There's salt in there. Careful though. Dylan filled it last night, so it'll be..." Her jaw dropped for a few seconds as she watched Wade lift it with one hand. "Heavy." She shook her head as Wade winked at her once again.

Damn the man and his winks. And strong arms. And knowing smile. And...

She was honest when she'd said she wasn't ready for him yet. She wasn't. She needed another few days at least to work up the courage to talk to him. Weeks even.

Heck, make that months...and only after there were at least a thousand miles or more separating them.

Chapter Two

"STOP FROWNING AT the poor boy, Leah. You'll give him a complex." Grams hung her red coat on a hook by the front door and set her boots on the drying rack.

Leah shrugged herself out of the giant coat she wore, toed off boots that belonged in the garbage, and searched for her Mukluks before remembering they were in the wash.

"Your feet are soaked. What are you doing wearing Dylan's old boots? They're too big for you, girl." Grams tsked as she stared at Leah's obviously wet socks.

"Too big and full of holes." Leah rummaged in the closet for an extra pair of slippers she was sure had been in there earlier. "I assumed Dylan would have kept all my winter clothes for me, but he apparently donated them."

"Go get some wool socks on then, for Pete's sake." Grams pushed her off toward the stairs, but Leah bypassed them and headed for the laundry room. First, she dumped all the clothes in the dryer in an empty clothes basket, then she fished through said clothes for a pair of thick wool socks she remembered seeing earlier. After pulling them on and sighing with relief, she pulled everything from the washer, put it in the now-empty dryer, and then turned it on, praying that her Mukluks would be okay. She'd never actually washed them before, so she had no idea if they'd survive the heat or not.

Guess she'd find out soon enough.

"Would you like a cup of tea? I'm sure the kettle is still hot," Leah asked, projecting her voice as she headed down the hallway. "The last thing you need is to get hit with a cold."

Grams had already poured water into a teacup and was dipping a tea bag into the water while petting Jack. The cat lay on the counter, his purr louder than a damn train whistle.

Leah scowled at the cat and swore the furry thing winked back at her.

"Why are you out and about on a morning like today?" Leah asked. "You should be back in your apartment, snuggled beneath a throw and watching your soap opera."

"As if I'm going to let a little cold weather keep me in doors. I had a craving for a muffin and all they had for breakfast was oatmeal and toast." A frown settled on Grams' face as she reached for one of the muffins Leah had made earlier.

Leah knew that wasn't true. "What was wrong with the fruit salad or a smoothie?" There was always an assortment of foods to choose from at Kindred Place, the local retirement home located in one of Marietta's Victorian houses.

"I didn't want a fruit salad or a smoothie. I wanted a

muffin. Specifically, the muffins your brother told me you've been making." Grams gave her a pointed look.

"So you're only here for my baking, is that it?" There was an unmistakable challenge in Leah's voice, one that egged Grams to deny what they both knew.

Grams chuckle admitted defeat. "For the record, as long you're staying, I expect fresh baking every morning."

Every morning? That wasn't so bad. "Deal."

"I also expect to see you every morning as well. Enough of this hiding here at home," Grams added.

Every morning? That was pushing it.

"I'm not hiding." Leah turned before she could see the disbelief on her grandmother's face and reached for a few plates from the cupboard. "Would you like a cinnamon bun?"

"You are hiding, and you know I would. Doctor says I need to add some weight to these old bones."

Leah chuckled. "I'm not, and I'm more than happy to oblige." Two could play that game.

"You really shouldn't be arguing with me, child. It's not fair to this old woman. Besides, you know you'll never win."

Leah kept her mouth shut as she led Grams to the kitchen table. Her grams might appear frail, but she was anything but.

Sure, she was petite. About the same height as Leah, Grams was half her size, and that wasn't saying much. Soaking wet, she probably only weighed about seventy-five pounds. The woman was skin and bones, yet she was as healthy as a horse.

"Why don't you go see how Wade's coming along?" Grams sat and licked her lips at the cinnamon bun. "I'm sure he'd like a piece of your buns as well."

Leah loved that Grams' eyes twinkled with laughter, but hated that the laughter and twinkle were directed at her. "The only buns of mine that man wants are the ones I bake in the mornings, and you know it." She rolled her eyes at her grandmother's obvious pun.

"I've never met a more obtuse and blind woman as you when it comes to that man. It's plain as day how much he loves you, but you can't see it, can you?" The disgust in her grandmother's voice wasn't something she was prepared for.

"Grams…" Leah started.

"Don't you 'Grams' me. I may be old, but I'm not blind. If anyone is, it's you." Grams' lips pinched together tighter than the zipper on her coat. "Go on now. It's the least you can do when he's out there clearing your sidewalk."

Leah didn't move. She wasn't quite ready to face Wade yet. She'd kind of hoped she could avoid him the whole time she was here, truth be told. She didn't plan to stay long, just until things died down a little and reporters weren't hounding her about her *confession.*

"Why did you bring him with you today?"

With that one question, Grams' countenance changed. Gone were the zipper-tight lips. Gone were the rigid shoulders and corset-laced straight back. Grams hunched her body forward with a slight tilt, heaved a sigh that would have blown out a dozen candles, and just shook her head.

"Is it a crime to want to see my granddaughter? You've been home for a day and not even a word. Dylan had to tell me you were here."

A knot of guilt settled within Leah's heart. She reached across the table for Grams' hand and squeezed it gently. "I know and I'm sorry. I was going to come see you, I promise. But you should have called. Dylan will be home soon and could have picked you up on his way home…or not…" Leah tried to backpedal her way out of that comment, knowing she was about to get a talking to from the look on her grandmother's face.

"Leah Morgan. I am not, nor have I ever been, a woman who gets *picked up*, thank you very much. I've got two legs that do me just fine. I'm not a frail old bitty who needs special handling. If I wanted to go for a walk to see my granddaughter, then that is exactly what I'm going to do." Grams' lips pursed together in one thin line, the red lipstick bright against her pale skin tone.

"And if you fall and break your neck? What then?" Leah attempted to reach out to pet Jack, but the way he looked at her had her changing her mind.

Truth be told, Grams might not be frail in spirit, but she was inching her way toward eighty years. Walking on icy sidewalks wasn't smart.

"Well then, I guess you're just gonna have to come with me. Aren't you?" Grams continued to pet the traitorous cat who arched his back beneath her hand.

"If we're talking early morning walks, then I'm in. As long as it's not too cold out." Leah averted her gaze while she sipped her tea.

"Why are you home? And without a word to anyone? Dylan said you wanted some time alone, but that doesn't make any sense to me."

"Would you believe me if I said I just wanted to get away from California for a few days?" Leah wasn't surprised at Grams' snort.

"Or that I was missing you and wanted to spend time with you?" Leah tried again.

Grams crossed her arms over her chest.

Guess not.

"I just needed to get away," Leah finally admitted. That was as close to the truth as she could handle right now. Every time she thought about what had happened, she was filled with anger, remorse, humiliation, and regret.

"Who or what are you hiding from, girl?" Grams asked her point blank.

Leah's heart spiked and her hands slightly shook, but she didn't answer.

Grams' brows rose with surprise. "Well now, I guess you are running from something." She patted her hand. "Is there something you need to get off your chest, love?"

Leah swallowed hard. She wanted to tell Grams everything, confess the mistake she'd made, the consequence of her actions...but Wade was outside. Considering he was the reason she was here, so to speak, the last thing she wanted was him walking in and overhearing the conversation.

"Did something happen at work?"

Leah shook her head, then stopped. The slight shrug of her shoulders had Grams pursing her lips and giving her that *don't-make-me-draw-this-out-of-you* look.

Leah bit her lip, glanced over her shoulder quickly to make sure Wade hadn't come in without her noticing, and then sighed.

Heavily. With enough exaggeration to have her grams pull her into a tight hug.

Tiny pinpricks of tears sent stabs of pain through Leah as she tried really hard not to cry.

Really, really hard.

"Oh love, what is going on?" Grams pulled away and gently wiped the few tears that had trickled their way down her cheeks. "It's not that garbage I read online, is it?"

Startled, Leah pulled back. She hadn't expected anyone in Marietta to have read that stuff yet, let alone Grams. She thought she had time still...

Ohgod-ohgod-ohgod-ohgod-ohgod. She couldn't breathe. If her grams knew, then the whole retirement home knew, which meant Wade knew, which probably meant everyone in this godforsaken little town also knew.

No wonder he hadn't called, texted, or sent her a smiley face on Facebook.

No wonder Dylan seemed dodgy when he came home last night when she'd asked if he'd heard any whispers about what she'd done.

No wonder her grandmother was here right now. *Going on a walk, my foot*, Leah thought. Grams had come here to make sure Leah was okay.

And Wade knew.

She was a fool.

"Please tell me you did not go on that reality television show to find a husband when you had someone waiting here at home, did you?" Arms on her hips, Grams gave her the fiercest frown she'd seen in a long time.

It kind of scared her, truth be told.

"I did not go on national television to find a husband." Leah looked Grams right in the eye.

She wasn't lying. She really hadn't gone on that reality show for a husband; it was more of a favor for a friend so she didn't lose her job.

That worked out so well for her too. Every time Leah stepped in to save Betsy's butt, she always ended up burned… One day, she'd learn her lesson.

"Well, thank the good Lord for that!" Grams raised her hands in the air, reminding Leah of Sunday morning worship.

God wouldn't strike her down for telling a half-truth,

would he?

"That's what I told the girls, but you know them…if it's in the news, it must be true. Silly group of gossips, if you ask me." Grams shook her head with apparent disdain while Leah felt absolutely sick to her stomach.

She was going to throw up.

"As if my girl would do something so foolish," Grams continued, oblivious to the way Leah's face blanched.

She shouldn't have come home. Listening to her big brother had been a mistake. She should have flown to Tahiti and spent the next few weeks in complete oblivion on the beach. There was still time. It didn't have to be Tahiti. It could be anywhere…as long as it was outside the United States.

"Why would they make up lies like that?" Grams asked.

"Well…it's not so much that the papers lied, but that they didn't tell the whole truth." Like a little child waiting for the scorn of disapproval, Leah's shoulders hunched and she couldn't quite meet her grandmother's gaze as she said the words as quietly as she could.

"What's that? Speak up, girl. I'm not getting any younger."

Leah winced.

Grams sighed.

They were quite the pair, weren't they?

"No. I don't want to hear it. Not right yet. I have a feeling I need fortification for this news, and the tea isn't going to cut it. That boy of yours should be close to done, and I'm in the mood for hot chocolate." Grams lips thinned until they were straight lines. "Do you know what he told me on our walk here?"

Leah shook her head. "What's that?"

"That despite being home now for a good solid day, you hadn't said a word to him. Normally, he's the first one you call when you land." Grams tsked. "It's why I brought him. I figured you must be fighting. If so, it's time for you two to make up."

Leah rolled her eyes. If only they'd been fighting.

"I saw that. Now go see how Wade is doing."

Despite wanting to do anything but go see how that man outside was doing, Leah made her way to the living room and watched him through the front window.

Wade was bent over, his shoulders hunched up to his ears as he shoveled the snow in front of the house. "He looks so cold out there," she muttered.

"Nonsense." Grams sneaked up behind her. "That boy doesn't like to keep still. His idea of relaxing is shoveling the walkways. He was at Kindred Place early this morning. Kathy, the head cook, mentioned he'd already cleared a pathway for her from her cottage."

Leah's brow raised. "He finds that relaxing?" That would be the last word she would have used to describe snow shoveling. Tiresome, cold, exhausting, freezing, time consuming, bone chilling, hard work...those would be her words.

Grams placed her hand on Leah's back. "Says it gives him time to gather this thoughts. His daddy was like that, too. A man of few words but full of action."

Leah could barely see the man outside, with the way the wind had picked up and blew the snow around in a haphazard way.

"Oh, he's no man of few words, trust me." Leah had always loved that about Wade. He gave off the whole strong-but-silent-type vibe but that man knew how to articulate his thoughts and feelings quite well.

She'd ran hard and fast away from Marietta...and away from him more than ten years ago because he'd broken her heart. She'd thought they were in love, that their relationship was one of the pure ones. Sure, they weren't officially dating, but everyone knew they were together. At least, she'd thought they were. She'd thought they were soul mates. Yet, she'd found out through high school gossip that he'd slept with Amy Pickerson, the most popular girl in school.

She'd been devastated. Destroyed. Their relationship forever damaged.

So she'd ran. Found a job as a traveling nanny for the summer with the woman who'd created KIND, the charity Leah had eventually started working with.

After a few months of nursing her broken heart, she let Wade explain what happened. It'd all been a lie, spread after he'd turned Amy Pickerson down when she asked him on a date. But the damage had already been done. It took a few years to salvage their friendship, and now…well, she was lost without him in her life.

She'd told him that last month. Well, she'd actually told him she loved him, and then waited for him to say those words back.

And waited.

Until it was obvious he wasn't going to say them back.

What he did say was he had to leave for a trip and would be out of range for about a week, but that he wanted to talk about it when he got back.

Basically…thanks-but-no-thanks-we-did-this-before-and-it-didn't-work-remember?

What she wouldn't give to turn back time. She felt like she was living Cher's song…over and over and over.

After that pitiful conversation, Leah's life went into a tailspin. She'd been asked…no, make that begged. Betsy, her best friend, had begged her to come onto the reality show after one of the girls had backed out last minute. Leah hadn't wanted to, but it had seemed like a good excuse at the time to ignore her broken heart.

She had a hard time saying no to Betsy. She knew it. She didn't have a hard time saying no to anyone else, but when it was Betsy… Well, the guilt of the one time she'd said no was too heavy a burden to carry.

They were roommates then. After a really rough day at work, all Betsy had wanted to do was go to a bar and drown her sorrows.

Normally, when Betsy went to the bar, Leah was there as a support. She was the driver, the caretaker, the shield against those who wanted to take advantage of her gorgeous but drunk friend.

This one night, Leah hadn't wanted to go. She'd just come back from a tour of high schools, and the stories she'd heard from the students who'd lost their parents, siblings, or friends due to drunk drivers was still too heavy on her heart. All she'd wanted to do was climb into a hot bubble bath with a good book and then sleep for a week.

So Betsy went alone.

At three in the morning, Leah was woken by her phone. She'd missed five phone calls from Betsy throughout the night. This call was from the police.

Betsy had been drugged and raped that night.

Leah blamed herself. If only she'd gone. If only she'd been there to watch over her friend, to protect her…

Betsy never blamed her. Not when Leah rushed into the hospital room and found her friend lying on a bed, curled tight in a blanket. Not when they sat on the couch in silence while watching mindless comedy movies. Not even when Betsy crumpled into a ball and finally sobbed in Leah's arms.

Betsy never once said *if only*…never once.

But Leah lived with that guilt. And because of it, she couldn't say no. Not again. Not when it came to her friend.

So when Betsy begged Leah to come onto *Charmed*, the

reality show where love conquered all…as much as she hated the idea, she didn't say no.

What was supposed to be a week of helping her friend turned into a month of torture with no way to contact the outside world. The moment she'd stepped into the hotel, her phone and computer had been confiscated. Betsy had promised it would only be for a few days, that she could leave right after the first rose ceremony if she'd wanted.

Oh, she'd wanted.

Looking back, if Leah hadn't admitted her feelings to Wade and he hadn't gone on that trip…none of what had happened would have happened. She wouldn't be here, hiding her bruised heart, wishing for the chance to go back in time.

She never should have gone on that show.

But truth be told, whether she'd confessed her feelings to Wade or not, she probably would have.

Because Betsy asked.

Things would have turned out differently though. She wouldn't have been betrayed by her friend, taken advantage of by the show, or made a fool of all because she'd confessed her broken heart on national television.

Leah needed to remember those feelings of shame and regret for the next time he gave her that knee-weakening-toe-curling-spine-tingling smile of his again.

"I'll wrap up a cinnamon bun for him. That's the least I can do for him clearing the sidewalk." Leah turned her back toward the window after Wade had glanced up and caught her watching him.

"Oh for Pete's sake." Grams threw her hands up in the air. "Why don't you join Wade and me for hot chocolate? Don't bother offering to make me some here, I know that garbage your brother keeps in his cupboard. Come have a cup of Sage's hot chocolate with us."

Grams' request was more like a demand, and they both knew it.

All Leah wanted to do was head back to bed, pull the covers over her head, and wish for the day to start over.

Heading out in public, having to show her face after her public humiliation…not really something on her need-to-do-today list.

Especially if the local gossip was already growing.

Grams headed toward the front door where she grabbed her coat. "I realize you're hiding from him for some reason, but what you and Wade have isn't to be thrown away. There's nothing stronger than the bond of friendship, Leah. Nothing. So go on now, grab some proper boots, and I'll tell Wade we're almost ready to go."

Leah bunched her lips together in what she hoped her grams took for a smile. She was quite content to let her think they were arguing. That was so much better than the truth. But, to be honest, spending time with Wade was the last thing she wanted to do at this moment and Grams knew it too.

"You know, Grams. I think I preferred our relationship when there were states separating us rather than mere houses. You were less…demanding." She took the jacket Grams held in her hands and helped her grandmother put it on.

Once the jacket was buttoned all the way to her grandmother's slim neck, Leah found herself wrapped in a tight hug. "Demanding and yet you love me. There's a reason you came home, Leah girl."

Leah swallowed back the lump that swelled in her throat.

"My heart is yours, you silly old woman," Leah whispered before pulling back and staring up toward the ceiling, banishing any hint of tears that would have appeared if she looked into her grams' eyes.

"You say that now, but your heart is fickle," Grams teased. "I know the minute we walk into that chocolate shop you'll be lured away by another love."

Leah chuckled, quite happy to turn the conversation away from her love life.

Kneeling down, Leah was focused on helping her grandmother step into her boots. "It's true," she said. "I've only ever had one true love—" She lifted her head and noticed Wade stand within hearing distance.

For Pete's sake…

She hoped he hadn't heard her, but the way his head angled toward the house and the widening of his eyes, she knew he had.

Slowly, Leah straightened and gave her sweet, *frail-but-*

stubborn-as-a-mule grandmother a sharp look.

The gleam of mischief in Grams' eyes was too much. Too. Much.

"Don't play matchmaker, please," Leah begged quietly as Grams stepped past her and onto the front porch.

"Oh love, I'm not playing." Grams winked before reaching for Wade's outstretched hand, which was meant to help her down the stairs.

With a very weary sigh, Leah closed the door behind her as she followed.

There were a lot of things Leah was afraid of. Heights, spiders, bees, public humiliation…just to name a few. But her grams' love for matchmaking was at the top of the list.

Leah could count on one hand the times Grams' matchmaking schemes had failed in the past. That was how good her grandmother was.

Chapter Three

THE TEN MINUTE walk to the Copper Mountain Chocolate shop took forever.

With Grams at her side talking incessantly about absolutely nothing and Wade trailing behind them, Leah felt each of those seconds stretch on until she was sure they'd never end.

Each time they passed someone in the street or waved to someone standing at their window looking out, Leah would hunch her shoulders and readjust her scarf so no one would recognize her.

"So it's a plan then?" Grams nudged her in the side, a sly look in her eyes moments before she winked.

Leah didn't like that look. She didn't trust it. She'd seen that look in Grams' eyes all too often, and it always meant she was up to no good.

"You know I wasn't listening." Leah's face flushed…and not from the cold, biting wind either.

Wade chuckled behind them. She gave him a scathing glance over her shoulder while Grams tsked.

Wade stepped ahead of them to open the door into the shop. Immediately, the tantalizing aroma of chocolate wafted out the open door.

Leah breathed in deep the sweet smell. Her insides melted as the aroma of comfort hit home, and she couldn't wait to sip the decadent treat. Dylan had brought her home a cup of the hot chocolate along with a box of Sage's handmade truffles when she'd arrived. He'd warned her that after one sip, she'd never drink anything else.

He'd been right. One sip was all it had taken. How could she have forgotten how much she loved Sage's cocoa?

If only Sage would sell her delectable goodness in powder form so she could make it at home once she left here. She'd be the world's happiest woman.

Leah stomped the bright yellow rain boots she'd found in Dylan's closet on the matt and unbuttoned her jacket before joining Grams at a table. Wade had disappeared back outside, muttering something about clearing the sidewalk.

"I wish you two would hurry and make up. I never did like it when you were at odds," Grams said as she sat down.

Sage, the owner of the chocolate shop, came out from the kitchen area, tying on what looked like a fresh apron.

"Well, look who it is, Marietta's long-lost daughter. About time you came in to say hi." Sage walked out from behind the counter, arms opened wide to give Leah a hug.

"Good to see you, too." Now this was Karma at her finest...having connections with one of the state's best chocolate makers and being able to call her friend. "Dylan threatened to stop bringing your cocoa home for me if I didn't come in to see you."

"And so he should. This is normally the first place you come to when you get back in town, but what…how many days have you been home holed up in your brother's house?" Sage held on to Leah's shoulders, but rather than the condemnation or judgment Leah expected, she only saw compassion and friendship.

"Only one." Leah soaked in what Sage was offering, and it felt good. Especially after her fear of receiving the exact opposite treatment.

"One is too long." Sage pulled her in for another hug, squeezing tight before turning toward Grams.

"Now you are the last person I'd expect to see out in weather like this, Josie." Sage held open her arms to give Grams a hug, this time. "It's so good to see you though!"

"I was in the mood for a cup of your hot chocolate. Kathy keeps trying new recipes, but…" Grams shrugged before sitting down.

"So that's why Kathy called this morning. She mentioned something about trying to put a smile on a cantankerous old woman's face, but I had no idea she was talking about you," Sage teased before she headed toward the back counter where her hot cocoa sat on a burner.

Leah followed Sage to the counter and watched as the woman stirred the drinking chocolate with a wooden spoon before filling two mugs.

"Don't you skimp on that whipping cream, you hear?" Grams called out.

"Never." Sage covered the large helping of whipped cream with fresh chocolate shavings before setting the two mugs on a tray.

"What would you recommend?" Leah couldn't stop eyeing the chocolate display. "I'm torn between your truffles or your mint melts."

"Try the truffles, considering I packed that box of chocolates with melts last night," Sage said.

Leah looked up in surprise.

"Oh, come on. How else did you think I knew you were home? Your brother only ever buys two things when he comes in. Hot chocolate and haystacks." Sage smiled. "I was hoping he was trying to impress a new date, but when I saw you walking with Josie and Wade, I figured he bought them for you."

"Does my brother often buy his dates chocolates?" Leah couldn't remember the last time Dylan told her he'd gone out with someone. He'd been engaged once, but he was left at the altar when his fiancé had gotten cold feet. But that had been almost ten years ago now.

"I don't think I've seen that brother of yours on a date in years." Sage handed Leah both a mint melt and a truffle, which she took willingly. "I think I'm a bit addicted to your melts."

"Your brother says the same thing when it comes to my haystacks. Speaking of him dating, don't you know anyone you could set him up with?"

Leah had just taken a bite of her chocolate when she paused, her hand slightly shaking. Did Sage know? Was that what she meant by her knowing anyone? Leah was just on *Charmed*, a reality television show with twenty other single women vying for the attention of one eligible bachelor. Obviously, she knew lots of somebodies, but…

The door to the shop opened, and Wade stepped in. "Sage, you're all out of salt. I'm going to pop over to Big Z and grab a bag. Sound good?"

Leah avoided the glance he gave her as she took the tray of hot chocolates to the table.

"That would be great, Wade. Thank you. When you're done, be sure to come in for a cup," Sage said.

When Wade closed the door, Sage came over with a small plate of chocolates.

"Where's Portia? Aren't you supposed to be in the kitchen making those delicious treats of yours?" Grams looked around the small shop with a frown.

"She has a doctor's appointment this morning, but she'll be in later." Sage busied herself with setting the plates on the table.

"Is everything okay?" The concern in Grams' voice startled Leah. What was wrong with Portia?

"I guess we'll have to wait and see." Sage gave Grams a

look full of misgiving and concern before forcing a smile on her face.

For a moment, Leah wanted to ask what was going on, but she bit her tongue. She had her own problems to deal with.

"That man of yours is pretty special." Sage winked before she headed back toward her kitchen area.

"He's not my man." Leah swallowed hard as she reached for her hot cocoa.

Sage laughed. "Oh honey, of course he is. Regardless of what I read in that article, we all know you two belong to each other. You always have and you always will."

Leah choked on the mouthful of cocoa.

"You read that garbage too, did you?" Grams frowned. "Why they'd print such trash is beyond me. Leah didn't go on that show and should sue for defamation."

Leah's eyes widened.

Sage frowned.

Grams looked alarmed. "You didn't go on that show. You told me so this morning," she clarified.

The words were right on the tip of her tongue, but Leah couldn't get them out, no matter how hard she tried.

"Of course she went on. It's all in the news and magazines, Josie." By now, Sage's brows had knitted together whereas Leah knew she had the face of a kid caught in the middle of a lie.

"What I said was I didn't go on the show to find a husband." Leah didn't look at either women; she couldn't. A knife twisted in her heart, the pain so awful all she wanted to do was run home and hide.

How could she explain to her grams why she'd gone on that show, especially when she'd known she shouldn't have, yet did it anyway? Or that she knew Wade wasn't *her man*, as Sage so deftly put it, primarily because when she admitted her feelings for him, he all but ran from her?

When Leah did manage to look up, Grams' eyes were closed but her lips were moving a mile a minute in what Leah could only assume was a prayer for patience.

"Leah, child. Would you please explain to me why you would go onto such a cheesy show and make a fool of yourself like you did?" Grams straightened in her seat and placed her hands in her lap, as if waiting patiently for Leah's answer, except Leah knew better.

Her grandmother never waited patiently for anything. If they weren't here, in Sage's shop, she'd be getting a major talking to that would no doubt leave her in tears. Grams hated half-truths more than she hated being lied to.

"I'm sorry, Grams." Leah lowered her gaze again.

"Don't apologize to me. I think you owe yourself and that man out there an apology. What were you thinking?" The disappointment in Grams' gaze twisted the knife in Leah's heart even more.

"I was thinking I was helping a friend. I was thinking it might help to get word out about my charity. I was thinking—"

"Sounds like you let that Betsy girl talk you into something you knew was a bad idea," Grams said, interrupting her.

Leah shrugged. That about summed it up.

"So you weren't on there looking for love?" Grams asked.

Leah shook her head.

"What about the things written about you?"

Leah sighed and reached for her cocoa. The taste was flat, almost bitter, but she knew that had everything to do with her mood and nothing to do with the cocoa itself. She pushed it away from her and stood.

"I'm going to head back home. Wade can walk you back, right?" She didn't want to stay here anymore. She couldn't.

The things written about her. They'd been hurtful. Mean. Mocking. They took one small scene, twisted by the producers to add more drama to an otherwise boring evening, and magnified it until it became all about her.

Lonely Leah.

She wanted to blame Betsy for what occurred that evening, but she couldn't. She had only herself to blame.

Yes, she'd gone on that ridiculous dating reality show. Betsy had called, asked for the favor of a lifetime, and Leah had said yes. She'd promised Leah would only need to stay for one night, and then she could walk away.

Leah's first instinct, of course, had been to say no. But when Betsy mentioned she'd make sure Leah got time to sit down with the eligible bachelor so she could talk about her story and her charity… Leah figured one night couldn't hurt, right?

Especially since she'd basically just poured out her heart to Wade about being in love with him and he'd turned away from her.

What a fool she'd been. For so many reasons. For admitting her feelings. For going on that show. For listening to Betsy. For drinking and letting things go too far.

"Don't run from me." Grams reached out for Leah's hand. "Sit, drink your cocoa and eat your chocolate. We'll deal with this. I don't understand a lot of things, but from the look on your face, I think you're punishing yourself enough."

Leah let Grams pull her back down to her seat. She wiped at the tears she hadn't realized had fallen and took another sip of her cocoa.

It wasn't so bitter this time.

"I might need another cup of this." The corners of Leah's mouth upturned into what she hoped resembled a smile. A fake smile, but a smile nonetheless.

"This is what love tastes like," Grams said.

Leah's brows furled. "Excuse me?"

"Didn't you notice the plaque on the counter? It's how they market their hot cocoa."

Leah twisted in her seat to look. Sure enough, a sign was on the counter.

"Wade happens to love the cocoa, too," Grams added.

"Don't."

One word. It was all Leah needed to say. *Don't. Don't push this. Don't force it. Don't try to fix what's already broken. Just don't.* She wasn't sure she and Wade could get past what happened. How would they remain best friends after what happened? It was bad enough she'd poured out her heart to him and he rejected her, but then to do it on national television… She hadn't just made a fool of herself, she'd made a fool of him, too.

Thank God she'd never said his name. It was only a matter of time, though, before the media figured it out and started harassing him.

He'd never forgive her.

"There is nothing you could have done that can't be forgiven."

With the precision she had once been known for when it came to darts, Grams unknowingly threw one aimed dead center at Leah's heart.

Leah had come home with two fears.

Ruining everything with Wade, and Grams never forgiving her.

No matter what Grams just said, not everything would be forgiven once she found out the truth. And if she read more of those magazine articles, she'd known the truth soon enough.

"After everything you've been through together." Grams

squeezed Leah's hand. "This is just another detour in the road toward your ever after."

Leah looked over her shoulder toward the front window where Wade stood outside talking to Paul Zabrinski, the owner of Big Z hardware. It almost hurt to look at him, knowing he was out of reach. Why, why, why had she screwed things like she had?

"Things aren't the same anymore, Grams." Leah sighed. "A month ago, I told him how I felt and he shrugged me off." Admitting that was hard.

Grams frowned. "You told him you loved him, and he shrugged you off? I find that hard to believe."

"Regardless, it's the truth." Leah stared up at the ceiling as her eyes welled up with tears. She would not cry. She would *not* cry.

Grams handed her a napkin. Damned if it didn't get wet as she dabbed at her eyes and cheeks.

"I do not want to cry, Grams. Please. Let's talk about something else, okay? Better yet, let's not talk. Drink your cocoa, and then I'll walk you home." Leah nudged Grams' cup toward her before taking a gulp of her own warm cocoa.

"Don't bother rushing me now. The key to enjoying this drink is to savor it, one sip at a time. You down that like it's chocolate milk and you cheat yourself of the experience Sage has worked hard to create." Grams shook her head with disappointment before she sipped her cocoa, giving Leah a pointed look as she did so.

Leah let out a long breath of air. She should know better than to rush her grandmother.

"What you need to do," Grams looked out toward the window and then back to Leah, "is talk to that boy and get everything out in the open. Maybe he didn't hear you. Maybe he misunderstood. Maybe—"

Leah barked out a laugh. "Oh, he heard me all right. Kind of hard to misunderstand the words I love you."

"And he didn't say it back?" Grams' eyes widened and her mouth opened into a perfect O shape.

Leah winced, shaking her head.

"That boy loves you more than life," Grams said after a few moments. "I know it. You know it. He for sure knows it. This doesn't make sense. Sit down with him, girl. Talk it out. This isn't a drawn-out romance story, for Pete's sake, where happily ever after could be possible after the first few chapters if only the author would make her characters talk. It's life. Life can get messy and muddy and everything in between, but as long as there's open communication between two people who love each other...anything can happen." Grams glanced back out the window, her mouth twisted and her forehead creased before she shook her head.

"If you don't talk to him, I sure will. I'll give him a good smack on the upside of the head while I'm at it, too," Grams muttered.

Ack! That was the last thing Leah wanted.

"You'll do no such thing. Let's pretend I said nothing,

okay? I'm only here for the week, just until things die down, and then I head back home to continue with my life. Hopefully, I'll still have a job to go back to." She whispered that last sentence.

She'd screwed up so many things in her life this past month, and she couldn't blame it all on *Charmed*. It had started when she asked Wade if there was still a chance for them—told him she realized she was in love with him.

If only she could go back in time.

Chapter Four

"WHAT IS WRONG with that woman?" Wade grumbled beneath his breath as he dug the shovel beneath a thick pile of snow, tossing it to the side. Leah had a way of getting under his skin, more so than any other woman he'd ever known.

It wouldn't take him long to work up a sweat, so he unzipped his jacket to mid-chest and pushed his shoulder blades back, enjoying the way his spine cracked with his stretch.

Wade glanced over at the chocolate shop and studied Leah as she sat with Josie.

She looked good. More than good, even bundled beneath that extra-large jacket and thick scarf. He'd wanted to wrap her in a big bear hug, but he'd refrained once he caught the scared look in her eye. She'd reminded him of a rabbit he'd snared during that last hiking trip.

Why would she be scared of him?

He thought everything was fine between them. Sure, they hadn't talked in a while, which was a bit uncharacteristic, but it wasn't unusual either. Leah had just returned from speaking at various high schools across the country, and he'd been about to leave to take a few city folks on a weeklong hunting excursion. Their conversation had been odd, and then with her in the bathtub and all... She wasn't upset with him about that, was she?

The whole time he'd been away, he'd had an inkling he was going to regret not calling her back. It was like an itch in the center of his back, right along the spine where he couldn't reach—annoying and persistent. They'd known each other long enough that...

He looked at her again, at the way she held the cup of Sage's hot chocolate between her hands. He'd known her long enough that he should have known to call her back.

Out of all the women in his past, she was the last one he'd call overly emotional, and yet...even Leah had her moments.

Like the time he'd sent her flowers for her birthday and they'd been delivered to the wrong apartment. When he'd called to wish her a happy birthday, she'd burst into tears because she thought he'd forgotten. Or the time he'd made her a scarf after being conscripted into one of the craft classes at Kindred Place by Josie, and she'd thrown her arms around him and declared it her favorite scarf. Granted, she'd been sick with a head cold at the time and the meds she'd been on made her a little...odd, but favorite? Even he knew that wasn't true. The thing had been long and full of holes, but he'd made it with her in mind. Despite living in California, she always complained of being cold. It wasn't like he expected her to wear it in public or anything.

Except she did. And was wearing it, even today.

He put all of his strength into piling more snow on his shovel and throwing it over his shoulder when he heard the honk of a truck behind him.

Wade turned and lifted his hand in greeting as his best friend, Josh Spencer, pulled up. Wade stepped over the mounds of snow against the curb and stepped close to the passenger door. A wave of hot air hit him as Josh rolled down the window.

"Almost done?" Josh was one of Marietta's snow angels and would run through town with the truck he'd attached a plow to in order to help keep the streets clean.

"Just another pass along the side streets. I'll hit Kindred Place and your house before heading home." Josh leaned his crossed arms on the dashboard and gave him a *you-won't-be-thanking-me* type smile.

Wade groaned. "I don't need another hill in front of my house." Last time it snowed like this, Josh thought it would be fun to build a tobogganing hill right beside his driveway. "Gonna bring your skates to the lake later? Maybe do a game of shinny?"

The excitement on Josh's face was answer enough. "I'll grab the boys, and you grab the beers."

Wade slapped the passenger door and stepped back.

"Deal."

By the time Wade had finished the sidewalks on both sides of the street, he was drenched in sweat. A few business owners had come out to say thanks, telling him to have a drink at Sage's place on them. Like he'd say no. Everyone knew how much he loved Sage's hot chocolate. In fact, he couldn't wait to head in there…not just for the hot chocolate, but also to sit with Leah and maybe catch up.

Damn, but he missed that girl.

He kicked his boots against the stone step before opening the door and calling out a greeting as he peeled off his jacket and hung it on the coat rack.

"Ready for your mug now?" Sage asked as she stepped out from the back, wiping her hands on her stained apron.

"You bet. I should have some credit still, right?" When he shook his head, droplets of water went flying everywhere.

"Wade, you could buy everyone in town a cup of my cocoa and still have enough left over." She handed him a chocolate melt as he approached the counter.

That was another he thing he loved about this place. Sage's chocolate melts. One bite was all it took to fall in love—not that he'd ever admit it or anything.

"You must be happy to have your girl home," Sage whispered after handing him his mug of cocoa.

Wade glanced over to the table where Leah sat.

Happy? Having his girl home meant more than that, even if Leah were only here for a short time. She might not admit it, but this was where she was meant to be, no matter what she said to the contrary.

Whenever anything monumental happened in her life, Marietta was where she ran to. Good, bad, or ugly, this was where she came to celebrate, to hide, or just to rest. She might claim to not be a small-town girl, and she sometimes complained about the hick life or her redneck upbringing, but, in her heart, this was who she was.

Montana born.

"One day, I'll convince her to stay."

Sage gave him one of her looks. The one that said *she'll-only-stay-if-you-share-your-heart*, and he just shrugged. She didn't know Leah like he did. He'd been there, done that, and went off to lick his wounds in the great outdoors for a solid week. They were better off as friends. At least, that was what Leah believed.

He'd convince her otherwise, one day, but until then, he'd be the best friend he could be, as much as that sucked. And sucked it did.

He wanted more from her. Not just best-friend status, but lovers as well. Husband and wife, soul mates, better halves, and everything that entailed. He wanted it all. Until she could give it, he'd take what he could get.

He was a patient man.

"Well, you're not going to convince her by standing here talking to me." Sage gave a pointed look toward Leah and Josie before she headed back into her kitchen.

Wade breathed in deep, placed a smile on his face, and pulled the empty chair at the table out and sat.

"It's about time you joined us." Josie placed her hand over his and squeezed. "I thought for sure you were planning on shoveling the whole town before joining us for a cup."

"And miss a chance to sip this cocoa? Never." Wade knew he was staring at Leah as he responded to her grandmother, but that didn't stop him. He liked to see the blush grow on her face while she studiously avoided his gaze.

Leah pondered her empty mug, as if she could read her future in the remaining droplets of cocoa.

All he wanted was for her to look him in the eyes, so it would let him know things were okay between them.

If there was one thing Leah was, it was stubborn. When she didn't look his way, he leaned back in his seat, stretched out his legs, and purposely nudged Leah's feet.

She looked up at him for a brief moment, her brows married together with…annoyance? But she didn't move her feet.

Interesting.

"What's on the schedule for the rest of the day?" The laughter in Josie's voice was unmistakable.

"Dylan says it's gonna clear up, so I'm planning to play a game of shinny or two later with a few of the boys."

The look on Josie's face at the mention of her grandson's name was priceless. It was a look between family pride and parental embarrassment.

"It would be nice if that boy got one day of weather right this week at least."

"Oh, I don't know," Wade said. "My daily winnings keep going up each day he's wrong, so I'm okay with it." He'd put himself down for a two-week stretch of Dylan getting the temperature wrong by three degrees. So far, he was on a roll.

Leah leaned forward. He knew he'd grabbed her attention—finally.

"You're winning, huh?"

Wade gave a relaxed shrug of his shoulder, attempting to pretend it meant nothing that she remembered their deal.

"How much are you up?" He could see her mentally calculating the amount in her head.

"Enough." He kept a straight face, forcing his lips not to make so much as a minuscule move, despite the fact he was roaring with laughter on the inside.

Leah leaned in closer. "How much?"

She had a tad bit of a competitive streak in her, which she let out every once in a while.

"Close enough." He'd let this ride a little while longer.

"What are you two talking about?" Josie asked.

Leah sat back and crossed her arms. Her lips turned into one of those sulking scowls he liked to tease her about.

Wade waited to see if Leah would explain.

"I'm waiting." Josie tapped her fingernails on the table, the tap-tap-tap sound only increasing the fierceness of Leah's glare.

"Our girl here doesn't much like it when I bet on her brother. I offered to take her to dinner in exchange, but when she found out how much I won last year, she upped the odds. She's a little demanding, this one," he nudged her with his boot, "and wants a weekend vacation rather than just a good steak dinner."

He wasn't sure if he'd ever seen Josie's brows rise so high.

"Where on earth would you go for a weekend away?" Josie looked from Wade to Leah.

This time, he groaned while a smile bloomed on Leah's face. He'd let her have this one.

"I'm taking the country boy to Napa for a weekend of wine and relaxation. And when I say I'm taking, I really mean he's paying." The way Leah's eyes sparkled... Man, she took his breath away.

There was silence, and then Josie hooted. When that woman laughed, it came from the depth of her belly. The sound of it was something between an owl and a croupy cough, and it filled the room.

"I'm not sure which is funnier." Josie wiped her eyes after catching her breath. "The idea of Wade relaxing or seeing him at a wine-tasting event." She reached out and squeezed Leah's arm. "I like it either way."

This time when Leah looked at him, there was no hesitation. No awkwardness. Just a bright, clear smile he knew and loved.

Loved. Before, the thought of loving Leah would hit him in the core and leave him scared as a new colt out on the ranch, but now, the idea was comforting, natural. He loved Leah and always would. Even if she didn't feel the same way.

Except, he knew she did, in a sense. The love between them was warm and worn, like a comfortable blanket wrapped around a lap on a snowy day. They were best friends. Once, he'd tried to see if they could expand their friendship and be more than just friends...but Leah had made it more than clear she loved him as a friend and only a friend.

"I relax." Wade pretended to be offended.

Both of their brows rose at his remark.

"I relax," Wade reiterated. He took a gulp of his hot cocoa, enjoying the warmth as it slid down his throat.

"What was the last book you read?" Josie asked.

"I picked up the new outdoor guide from the bookstore." Good book, too. He'd discovered some new hiking trails he needed to try out in the next few months. He could add them to his website for day trips.

Leah rolled her shoulders. "That's work related, Wade. You are a hiking guide, so you need to read those books. What was the last one you read for simple pleasure?"

That one was easy.

"The last Brams Linn book." Brams Linn and James Rollins were his favorite authors. He had a whole shelf in his living room with their books. There was nothing he loved more than to sit in front of the fire at night and read through them, enjoying Linn's thrillers or making notes of all the latest scientific nuts and bolts Rollins threw into his stories, checking them out himself to see if they were true.

They always were.

"You never read the gossip magazines in the grocery line either, right?" Josie's words were slightly muffled as she held her mug of cocoa in front of her face.

Leah inhaled sharply, and Wade knew right away what Josie was hinting at.

He searched Leah's face and knew now wasn't the time to talk about the latest gossip he'd read.

"Why would I read that garbage? I've got better things to do while I wait in line…like help little old ladies count their pennies." He purposely goaded Josie, giving Leah a chance to regroup.

"Why, I…" Josie flustered as she sought for the right words to counter him. "I do not count my pennies."

He shrugged, not bothering to argue with her. She counted her pennies, but only so she could make sure there was enough to buy a sucker for Linda Rowe, her neighbor. Linda loved suckers, but she refused to buy any since she was on a tight budget.

Leah's cell buzzed. Wade didn't think much of it until he caught the tightness of her lips and the way her hand hovered over the phone, as if hesitating to pick it up.

"Answer it if you need to," Josie said.

"It's just Betsy."

"Good, let me talk to her." Josie held out her hand.

Leah hesitated but hit the call button and handed Josie the phone.

"Betsy, it's Josie, love. How are you? You know I'm not too happy with you, right? Not after that stunt you pulled with my granddaughter…uh-huh…yes, I fully expect you to make it up to her…that's a good girl. Now, why don't you call her back later? Good. Oh, and Betsy…it's been too long since you've been up here for a visit. Time to change that, right? You've got my number, so use it sometime." She winked at Leah as she said it.

Josie listened in for a few moments and Wade pretended not to listen, focusing on Leah instead.

Leah just stared at her grandmother with a mixture of annoyance and… He couldn't quite read the other emotion.

"Are you okay?" he asked with as much gentleness as he could muster as he reached for her hands.

"I'm fine," she mumbled before she withdrew her hands from his and placed them in her lap. She carried a look in her eyes that was similar to a deer in headlights.

"What's wrong, love?" Josie handed her back the phone.

"Nothing." Leah pocketed her phone and pushed her chair back, jumping up. "I could do with some more chocolate. What do you think?" Without waiting for an answer, she fled toward the counter and focused on the treats Sage offered.

"What was that about?" The wrinkle lines in Josie's forehead deepened as she watched Leah leave.

"Your wrinkles are showing." Wade knew he shouldn't tease her, but he wanted to break up the tension created by the phone call.

"Dear boy." Josie's attention was back on him. "You should know by now never to mention a woman's wrinkles." She tsked and shook her head.

"There's a lot of things boys aren't supposed to mention about girls. For instance, the things you read in those gossip magazines." He leaned forward, elbows on the table, and gave Josie a disapproving look. "What did you mention that for, anyway?"

Josie sighed, a very deep and very long sigh that said he should really know better by now.

"My granddaughter has a habit of running from things she can't handle. You. This town. Now the things being said behind her back. If there's anything I've learned in my seventy-odd years, it's this…running away only creates new problems. It doesn't solve any."

"You can't make her face something she's not ready for." Wade understood Josie's logic. In fact, he even agreed with it, but that wasn't how Leah dealt with things. Making her face something she wasn't ready for did no one any favors.

"You pretending you don't know what's going on won't help either." Josie's finger wagged as she scolded him.

"I'm not pretending, Josie. I heard the nonsense—saw

what they put online. I'm biding my time. There's a difference." He stopped himself from saying anything further because Leah was headed back their way, a large box of chocolates in her hand.

"I couldn't pick just one or two, so I figured what the heck," she said as if that explained anything.

For the next few minutes, awkward silence reigned between the three of them.

"Listen, ladies." He nudged his cup toward the middle of the table and stood. "I should head back to Kindred Place and make sure the walkways are clear before I head out for my game. Leah…" He waited until she looked up at him and gave her a soft smile. "You good to walk Josie back?"

She nodded.

He leaned down and placed a gentle kiss on Josie's head before doing the same to Leah's. "I'll see you later?" He directed his question to Leah, sure she'd agree and tell him to come by whenever he was free.

Except she didn't. She shook her head and mumbled something he couldn't quite hear.

"Pardon?" He leaned down to her.

With her head bent toward her chest, she again mumbled something that sounded awfully like she was busy.

"So, that's a yes then? Great. I'll text you." He pretended he hadn't heard what she'd said. He wasn't going to take no for an answer. That awkwardness between them bothered him.

"I said no." She cleared her voice and spoke a little too loudly.

He stepped back. He wanted to pull her up and make her look him in the eye. Force her to explain what was going on, but he knew she'd only retreat further. And retreating was exactly what she was doing.

Those stupid magazines called her Lonely Leah. Yeah, he'd read them. He'd seen all the latest gossip and knew she was probably embarrassed as hell right now.

Too bad. *Suck it up, buttercup* was what he wanted to say.

"I see. I guess I'll catch up with you later then." Let her retreat. Let her think he was going to give her space.

Wade didn't know how long she was in Marietta.

He also didn't know the true story behind those gossip magazines.

There were a lot of things he didn't know when it came to Leah.

But he did know one thing. He was going to find out. He was going to do his best to not only help shield her from whatever she was hiding from, but also do everything in his power to make it right.

There was no way the things those magazines claimed were true. Leah didn't drink. Period. Nor would she have claimed something she'd never felt unless there was a reason. She wasn't in love with a country boy from Marietta. She also didn't hate the small town she'd grown up in, which were the things the media claimed she'd confessed while drunk.

"Wade?" Leah called out as he stepped away from the table.

He paused, covered his head with his hat, and took a deep breath.

Leah licked her lips, and he could see the struggle to find the right words in her eyes.

"Thank you."

He nodded. He wasn't sure if she was saying thank you for cleaning her walkway, for bringing Josie to her place, or for giving the space she needed.

"Anything for you," was all he said. He meant it, too.

Chapter Five

WRAPPED IN HER grams' hand-knitted blanket, an almost empty box of chocolates in front of her, Leah bawled like a baby as the credits rolled from the latest chick flick she'd found on TV.

She swiped her face with the long sleeve of her pajama top, popped another piece of chocolate into her mouth, and scrolled through the stations for another mind-numbing show to watch.

Leah didn't need to look at the clock to know she'd wasted the rest of her day lounging in bed, cocooned beneath the mound of covers, watching sappy movie after sappy movie.

She had the heap of discarded tissues to prove it.

When her cell phone buzzed, Leah jumped, tossing some of those tissues onto the floor.

She was half tempted to shut the phone off without looking to see who'd sent her a text, except her brother promised to bring her food home after his shift at the radio station, but only if she answered.

He didn't understand what the stress of keeping her phone on meant. Didn't see the messages from so-called friends wanting to check in on her, the notifications about the latest gossip site article calling her Lonely Leah.

God, she hated this person she'd become since that ridiculous show.

Since Wade turned her down, if she were being honest.

What happened to the strong, charismatic, independent woman she'd grown to become? Where'd she go?

She shouldn't be jumping because of a phone call. She shouldn't be scared to open her laptop and read the news feeds.

She should be confronting the issue. Placing blame where blame was due...except, she couldn't.

She had to keep her nose clean, her head down, and let things blow over. For the good of her job. For the good of the charity.

She wouldn't always be like this...right? So indecisive and...weak.

Pizza or Chinese? Dylan asked via message.

After all the chocolate she'd eaten, she didn't have much of an appetite.

Either one. Helllllooo, indecisive Leah.

Hot cocoa, too?

Leah snorted. She could answer that one easily. Didn't matter she'd drank three hot cocoas earlier today.

More chocolates too, please?

She also didn't really need more chocolate but…

What happened to the stuff I brought home yesterday?

Leah eyed the almost empty box—except this was the box *she'd* bought earlier.

Jack has an addiction you should get taken care of. I seriously don't think it's healthy for him to be eating chocolate. It's poisonous or something to cats, isn't it?

She wasn't sure if Dylan would buy the idea that his cat ate her chocolate, but it was worth a shot.

Rrriiight. Grams is joining us for dinner, so get out of bed. Don't bother arguing. I'm always right—you should know that by now.

Sure, she typed. *Rub it in my face.*

How did he know she was in bed? Some days Dylan scared her with how well he knew her.

He'd warned her not to go on that dating reality show. Warned her it would do more damage than good.

She wished she'd listened to him.

But of course, Leah thought she knew better. She'd let her best friend, who worked in the production crew, talk her into it. Betsy was always in crisis mode, and Leah should have remembered that.

But Betsy needed help and that was what Leah did best…helped others. Especially Betsy.

Always Betsy.

So, of course, she said yes.

It wasn't like she was there to fall in love.

In fact, she wasn't even sure she liked the bachelor, truth

be told.

But she'd also never expected to make a fool of herself on national television.

So here she was, in a town she never wanted to return to, with a career about to tank, curled up in a bed she hadn't slept in for years, and watching the sappiest movies she could find all because she didn't want to face reality.

She could have done that back home except when she'd pulled up into her driveway, cameras flashed while reporters harassed her for comments not only about the big revelation she'd admitted, but also about the fact she'd drank alcohol.

Not of her choosing, mind you. She'd been played.

Would *Charmed* ever admit that? Not in this lifetime. Betsy begged her to understand, to not rock the boat, and to just lie low.

Lonely Leah was what they called her in the tabloid and on the entertainment shows. At least it wasn't anything worse.

Lonely Leah who drank herself silly on national television and admitted to the world that she'd always been in love with a boy from back home.

What a fool she'd been.

She couldn't stay in Marietta long. She knew this. Once people got wind of the things she'd said and the confessions she'd made, she wouldn't exactly be welcomed back with open arms.

One did not just bad talk Marietta on national television

and get away with it.

She just needed the frenzy to die down. Her boss told her to lay low, to stay out of the news if she wanted to keep her job.

Leah rolled into a ball on the bed, arms clutched tight to a teddy bear that Wade, the one who'd stolen her heart years ago, had given her when she'd turned sixteen. She wished she could erase the past five days from her life.

She wished she'd never gone on that show.

She wished she'd paid attention to what she'd been drinking. They promised her it was pomegranate juice and club soda. She'd never have known it was really dessert wine and club soda. Of course she wouldn't have known. She'd never even taken a sip of alcohol before. Combine that with the fact she'd barely eaten anything all day, and it had been a recipe for disaster.

She wished she'd ignored the producers who asked her question after question after question about her lack of relationships until she broke down in tears, admitting the real reason why she never dated.

She wished a lot of things but, unfortunately, there was no wishing star available or magical cricket to make all her dreams come true.

If only life were like a fairy tale.

Not wanting to think about her humiliation any more, Leah forced herself out of her bed. She cleaned up, tossing all the tissues in the garbage, and then attempted to brush her knotted hair, giving up and placing it in a messy bun instead.

By the time she made it downstairs, her brother held the door open for Grams, who held a tray in her hands.

The look she gave Leah almost had her walking back up the stairs and hiding beneath her covers once more.

Almost.

Their walk back from the chocolate shop had been fairly quiet. Despite the plethora of questions Grams had peppered her with, Leah remained silent. Grams deserved answers, she deserved to know the truth, but Leah wasn't ready. She needed more time.

She'd walked Grams up to the retirement home but rather than invite her in, Grams had dismissed her, saying that Leah obviously needed some alone time. Grams had been hurt by Leah's silence—that much was clear. And Leah felt bad, she really did…but…not bad enough to apologize and confess everything.

The phone call earlier had unsettled her, to say the least. As did the seven text messages from Betsy begging her to return her calls and the forward from other friends about things being said online.

All she wanted to do was run and hide, pretend like none of this had ever happened.

Obviously, her grandmother had other things planned. If the thinned white lips didn't give it away, the solid stare said enough.

Leah was in the dog house with Grams, and being in that

proverbial dog house was never a good thing.

When she was little, her grandmother used to have a dog—a happy, excitable Sheltie that was spoiled worse than any grandchild had ever been. When they'd first got the dog, her grandfather had built a dog house in the backyard, complete with a chain that would leave enough room for the dog to roam in the yard.

When Grams had seen that contraption, she had one thing to say about it.

It wasn't large enough.

Her grandfather hadn't understood. For him, dogs belonged outside, but for Grams, her sweet little Sheltie would sleep at the foot of their bed and if he wanted to complain about it, well then, he could go sleep in the dog house and see how it felt. In fact, she even locked him outside that night after they argued about how much she spoiled that dog.

That Sheltie had never slept one night outside. Her grandfather couldn't say the same.

"Take this, will you?" Grams held out the tray that contained three coffee cups. Leah gladly took it and led the way into the kitchen where she started to set the table while her brother unloaded the bags of food in his hands.

"The food smells delicious," Leah casually mentioned, hoping to cut the obvious tension between them all.

Dylan gave a small shake of his head as he sat down at the table.

Leah waited until Grams had sat down before she followed suit.

She didn't like the atmosphere between them all. There was a coldness, an awkwardness she knew was her fault.

Three mouthfuls later, Grams tossed down her fork, breathed in deep, and broke the silence.

"I am not leaving tonight until you explain everything to me. And I mean everything."

Leah glanced at Dylan, who rolled his eyes in his I-told-you-so way he had down so well.

"Can I eat my moo shoo pork and egg rolls first?"

The frown on Grams' face deepened. "Don't get lippy with me. I let you off this afternoon, figured you needed time to sulk in private, but enough is enough."

"I wasn't sulking." Leah had watched sappy movies and balled like a baby instead.

The arch of Grams' brow rose to amazing heights and had Leah squirming in her seat.

"How about we all eat up and then we can have that family chat in the living room, okay?" Dylan offered his suggestion, one that Leah had no problem agreeing to.

She took her time eating her meal, one small bite at a time—anything to prolong the inevitable.

Betsy sent a few texts. After getting some pointed looks from her grandmother, Leah finally responded with a brief message.

Let's talk tomorrow. In a family meeting. I blame it on

you—just a FYI.

It's okay, Betsy texted back. *I deserve it. I'll make it up to you, promise. Talk later.*

Make it up to her? Leah wasn't sure if she liked the sound of that.

After all the excess food was put away and the dishes washed, the three sat in the living room, Leah curled up on the couch, Grams in the chair across from her, and Dylan lounged on the floor in front of the fireplace with Jack in his lap, purring louder than a freight train.

"How much of what I've read in the magazines is true?" Grams asked, not mincing words.

"About half." But half was enough.

Grams gave a deep nod. "So you weren't drunk then, right?"

Leah winced, hating having to admit the truth. "I was. There's no excuse. I should have known better. The producers had me sitting in the hot sun with no food and swore they were only giving me non-alcoholic pomegranate juice. They needed the 'bubbly' effect for the cameras. I was alone, tired, hungry, and…wasn't paying attention." She hated thinking back to that day.

She'd been forced to wear a bathing suit that revealed much more than she preferred and encouraged to swim and lie in the sun all day long, to work on her tan.

Leah didn't tan. She burned like a farmer's tomato, so she tried to stay in the shade as much as she could.

The other girls didn't talk to her much. They all knew she wasn't supposed to be there. Hell, everyone including the crew knew she wasn't supposed to be there. But, for some reason, the bachelor kept calling her name as he handed out the roses.

She wasn't sure why. In fact, one night she'd even declined to take it until Betsy came out and gave her big, sad eyes and begged her to stay one more night, for *her*.

Everything about this whole catastrophe had been for and because of Betsy.

"That doesn't explain why you stayed if you only agreed to one night," Dylan piped up.

"Betsy's job was on the line. She was low on the totem pole with something to prove and there were bets between the producers about whose girls would stay longer. They all thought Betsy's girls would be out first, and she wanted to prove them wrong. There's a bonus each week their girls stayed in…" Even as she said it, it sounded lame and made Betsy look money hungry. She wasn't, but Leah could see how it would look.

"I love that girl, I really do, but…" Grams rubbed her face. "Seriously, Leah, when is enough enough?"

Leah really had no response. This wasn't the first time Grams had said this. Heck, everyone in her life basically said the same thing and yet…she couldn't get out of the Betsy vortex.

"I've watched the show for years and didn't think any

harm would come of it. All the one-on-ones I spent with the bachelor, we talked about my past and my passions. I know I was able to spread word about the harm of drinking and driving and—"

"If they didn't edit it out." Dylan stretched and dislodged Jack from his lap. "I doubt any of that info will see any airtime. Trust me…if it doesn't suit their purposes, they're not going to show it."

"Betsy promised me they would." Leah needed to believe that. She had to believe that something good came out of all this craziness.

"I know you're a half-full type of person, but sometimes the cup is just half-empty." Dylan joined her on the couch.

"I can't believe they would get you drunk." Grams leaned forward, elbows on her knees. "Isn't there something you can do? Sue them or something…"

Leah shook her head. "I signed a contract. I also really don't want to put Betsy's job in jeopardy by saying anything bad, you know?"

"Not even if it means you lose your job? Does she care about that?" The chastisement in her brother's voice hurt.

"Of course she cares." Leah felt a strong need to defend her friend, despite everything that happened. "She promised to donate all the extra money she earned by me staying on to KIND." That was enough. It had to be.

By the look on her family's face, they didn't think it was.

"So the humiliation, the reporters staked outside your

house, the nickname the media gave you, hiding here at home—that's all worth it to you then?" Dylan challenged her.

Leah pulled up legs, drawing her knees tight to her face and rocking herself slightly. "No." That one single word tore out of her with an agony she tried hard to ignore. The tears gathering in her eyes were honest and heartfelt, and a small part of her wanted to rail on her best friend for placing her in this situation. Okay, a large part of her but...

"What can we do to help?" Grams asked. Her voice was laced with both concern and determination. In that moment, Leah loved her more than life.

"You need to counteract everything the media is saying. They're calling you Lonely Leah, so prove to them you're not." Dylan stood and stepped toward the living room window, pulling the curtains aside to look out.

"How exactly do you propose I do that? They're calling me Lonely Leah because of what I confessed while drunk. I can't exactly ignore that or pretend it didn't happen."

"How did they find out, anyway?" Grams asked.

Leah puffed out a breath of air. She wished she knew. Betsy swore she didn't tell. The contestants had no access to the outside world, so best Leah could imagine, one of the other producers or staff members had blabbed. Except, she didn't understand why.

It wasn't like the show was boring and they needed to create interest in the bachelor. He'd been on one of the previous seasons and had been well loved. The girls vying for his love fell all over him, and the amount of catfights and emotional breakdowns were plenty to keep viewers interested. Why they would focus on her...she couldn't understand it.

"I wish I knew. I really do. Maybe it was a slow gossip week and they needed something, anything, to fill papers with."

"It sounded orchestrated to me." Dylan massaged his chin. "Almost like they planned this to happen. Placing you in the sun, not giving you food, plying you with alcohol...you were a scene waiting to be played. Someone there didn't like you and wanted you to go down in flames."

"Maybe they won't play it when the show airs." Grams sounded almost hopeful.

Leah snorted. "Oh, they'll play it all right. No one's mentioned it yet, but the speech I was given during the rose ceremony was scripted. It'll be good ratings—small-town-tea-tottling-country-girl-sloshed-out-of-her-mind... There's no way they won't play that up." She buried her head in her hands, remembering the exit interview she was forced to do.

Grams pushed herself up from the chair and sat down beside Leah, reaching for her hand as she did so. "By the time it airs, all of this will have been forgotten about. Until then, we'll do what we've always done, stick together as a family." She squeezed hard.

A large pit dropped in Leah's stomach as she caught the

glint in Grams' eyes. She knew what that meant. Grams was already scheming.

"First things first, you need to stop hiding." By the way she nodded her head, Leah knew Grams expected her words to be truth.

Except they weren't. Not for Leah. Hiding was all Leah wanted to do.

"You don't understand, Grams." She never would either—not unless Leah confessed everything to her.

"It wasn't just that I got drunk and confessed all the deep dark secrets in my heart…" She winced at the memory of that moment, when she sat in that tiny room, surrounded by cameras and lights and the producers across from her who kept barraging her with questions, one after another, without giving her time to really think about what she was saying…

"Like saying how in love you are with Wade?" Grams asked.

Leah had a small coughing fit, choking on her words as she did so.

"Like that's really news." Grams rolled her eyes. "It was all everyone could talk about this morning over breakfast." She shook her head. "Darling, if you think anyone in this town would be surprised to learn about that, you're living in a dreamland. We've all known you two were meant for each other, ever since you were kids."

"We already discussed this, remember?"

Grams' brow furrowed as she looked at Leah with disapproval. "If you are insinuating anything about my memory or my age, you'd better think twice before you say anything else." Grams was definitely irked. "Of course I remember. I also remember you telling me there was no hope. But there is. There's always hope. I, for, one will never give up on you two."

Leah gave her grandmother a soft smile that said more than she could put into words.

Thank you. I appreciate that. At least someone has hope. I'll always love you for believing in us. She meant it all.

Josie seemed to have understood because she gave Leah's hand two pats before she stood.

"Now, it's time for tea and I promised the girls I would be there tonight. Leah, I expect to see you bright and early tomorrow with some of your home baking. The girls are going to hound you with questions, but you hold your head up high and tell it like it is."

Taken aback, Leah shook her head no several times. "I can't...you don't understand..."

Why was it that whenever she tried to tell the whole story, her grandmother would take one small piece of information and assume it was all she needed to know?

Grams placed her hands on her hips. "Then spit it out."

"I didn't just say I wasn't there for the bachelor or that..." She wanted to choke on her words again to stop them for being said. "Or that..." She couldn't do it...couldn't repeat that she'd been in love with Wade forever and only just realized it...too little, too late.

Grams whisked her hands in the air. "Yes, yes, that you are in love with Wade. Spit it out, dear."

Leah bit her lip and looked to Dylan for help.

"Oh no, you're on your own for this one." He held up his hands in mock surrender.

Leah leaned her head back and stared up at the ceiling, unwilling to watch the effect of her words on her grandmother's face.

"I said I was in love with Wade, but he lived-back-home-and-would-never-leave-the-town-I-never-wanted-to-return-to." The words rushed out, jumbled all together in hopes Grams didn't quite hear it all.

When there was no response, Leah dropped her gaze and slowly looked toward her grandmother.

Grams clasped her hands tight to her chest. "You criticized Marietta? On national television? Oh Leah, how could you?"

And there it was. Another one of her unpardonable sins.

No one talked down Marietta. No one. Especially not someone born and bred here. That was just not done. It was one thing to want to leave as a young adult, to desire to explore the world and expand one's horizons...but to publicly say you never wanted to return...

That just wasn't done.

"Dylan, love, take me home, will you?" Grams held out her shaking hand toward Dylan, her face ashen, her body stooped.

In all her years, Leah had only seen Grams look…old…a few times in her life. At her parents' funeral, at her grandfather's funeral, and when Grams' best friend, Linda, found out she had Alzheimer's.

"Grams…" Leah rushed over to her grandmother and wanted to give her a hug, to apologize, to express just how sorry she truly was, but she didn't. She hugged her body as she stood awkwardly in the hallway, watching Dylan help Grams get her coat on.

"Tomorrow, Leah. We'll…we'll deal with this tomorrow." The sorrow etched on her grandmother's face had tears pooling in Leah's eyes.

She would survive being a national embarrassment on television.

She would survive losing her job if it was what happened.

She would even survive remaining friends with Wade when she really wanted more.

But what she couldn't survive was knowing how much she'd disappointed the one person in the world who meant so much to her.

"It'll be okay," Dylan mouthed as he held the door open.

Leah shook her head.

She wasn't so sure it would be.

Chapter Six

WADE'S FINGER HOVERED over the send button.

Why was he hesitating? It wasn't like he was asking Leah to the prom or out on a date.

Well, technically, it would be a date but, he didn't get why this was so hard.

The last time she'd come home, he'd sent a similar text message to her and there'd been no issues, so why now?

Of course, the last time she'd come home, he'd met her at the airport and they were tied to the hip for the majority of her visit. Considering she'd never even told him she was here this time, he shouldn't be expecting anything to be the same.

Grab your mitts. The moon is bright, I've got a thermos of cocoa, and a new pair of binoculars.

If there was one thing Leah begged him to do every time she came home, it was wildlife watching during a full moon.

He hit the button and sent the message. Now all he had to do was wait.

What was going on with her? He couldn't put his finger on it. It was like she'd pulled away from him, but he wasn't sure why.

He'd sent her multiple text messages, emails, and even filled up her phone with voice messages after coming back from his trek into the woods. Now he understood why she'd never called him back.

She'd gone on that ridiculous reality show.

When he'd first heard about it, he'd headed to Grey's Salon and did the one thing he hadn't done in years. Ordered a beer. He'd let that beer sit in front of him until it grew warm. By the time Dylan showed up, he'd pushed the beer away and ordered suicide wings—killing not only his taste buds but also any sense of feeling in his body.

He'd fallen in love with Leah when they were silly kids romping around the countryside in snowshoes.

He'd fallen harder in love with Leah in high school as he watched the girl of his heart turn into a woman.

He'd fallen even further in love with Leah after they'd reconnected following the stupid breakup of theirs where she ran. It took a bit, but their friendship had deepened after that.

He knew then there was no one else he would want to be with.

She was it. She was everything. She was his home.

He checked his phone for a reply.

Checked it again fifteen minutes later.

She couldn't be asleep already; she was a night owl like him, so either she didn't have her phone close by or she was

CHARMED BY CHOCOLATE

avoiding him.

After everything about today, he tended to think it was the latter.

She'd said she wasn't ready for him.

Since when did she need to be ready?

Since when did it matter?

Before he could give it a second thought, Wade had his boots on and was out the door and in his truck.

Her bedroom light was on. Wade did what he'd done for so many years—he took a handful of small rocks he kept in the backseat cup holder, cupping them in the palm of his hand and tossing them toward her window.

The first few fell flat, but the fourth rock hit the window with a solid ping.

He lobbed another one in the air and heard the satisfying sound before there was a flutter to the curtain.

He lifted his hand in greeting, fully expecting Leah to open the window or at least give him a sign she was coming down.

Having the light turn off without so much as a glimmer of her silhouette…that was unexpected.

He tossed more rocks. Maybe he'd imagined the flutter of the curtain. Maybe he'd just missed her leaving the room, so he leaned against his truck and waited, giving her time to come down the stairs and meet him.

It irked him when she never showed up.

Wade liked to think of himself as a simple man. He

wasn't hard to figure out, wasn't the type to play games, tried to respect other's space and time, but Leah…when it came to her, he was as twisted as a ball of twine.

They'd once promised to be completely open and honest with each other, regardless of the situation. How she was acting right now…it didn't make sense. It was like she was embarrassed, unsure, questioning their relationship. But why?

He could count on one hand the number of times she acted like this toward him.

When her parents died and she froze.

When she thought he'd slept with someone else.

When she started to date that douche bag in California, which thankfully only lasted a few months.

When he told her he loved her.

That one still ate at him. On one hand, he wished he could take it back, that he'd refrained from sharing his heart and waited…but, on the other hand, he wasn't one to play games and she needed to know where he was at.

He still dreamed about that night. Woke up sweating from the outcome.

He used to text her afterward, just to make sure things were good between them.

So why did he stop?

Her window was still black.

Did he push her or pull back?

Pushing never worked out for him. Maybe it was time to

learn his lesson.

Wade climbed into his truck, but he didn't start it. He was torn.

He couldn't handle the space between them again. It was one of the reasons why he promised he'd never tell her he loved her again, not unless she said it first.

He'd surprised her one night after she'd finished speaking at a high school assembly in Spokane. It was only a six-hour drive or so, and he knew she wasn't flying out until the next day, so why not? Right?

The look on her face when she noticed him at the back of the assembly made that long drive worthwhile.

The hug he'd received once they were alone confirmed it.

They went out to eat and then went for a walk through a park, stopping for coffee along the way.

He'd thought things had been good.

He'd thought he'd read all the right signs. So, he took her hand and entwined his fingers through hers. She seemed a little stiff at first, but she'd eventually relaxed as they continued their walk.

It didn't take a lot of courage to pull her into his side. It felt right. It felt comfortable. They walked as they had for years, close.

The moment he looked into her eyes and told her he loved her, everything changed.

She pulled back. Away. Retreated within herself and wouldn't open up to him.

She begged him not to do it—not to ruin what they had. She'd seen it happen too many times to others and couldn't bear to lose him, not again.

He told her she never would, but she hadn't been listening.

So he did the only thing he could.

He stepped back. He erased the tension within his own body, ignored the way his heart bled, and continued their walk. Nothing was said for the longest time. He knew she was trying to read him, trying to find the right words to turn back time, but he didn't need to try to read her. He knew exactly what needed to be said.

"You'll never lose me. I'll always be right here, the one who knows you best. The one who loves you most. But if I can only have your friendship, then that will be enough." It tore at him to say the words he'd never wanted to say. It destroyed him to know that there would always be something missing, something between them...that there could have been more, but she was too afraid to even try.

But he couldn't lose her. Not then. Not now. Not ever.

He'd made her a promise before dropping her off at her hotel.

He would never tell her again how he felt, not like that, not until she was ready and not until she said it first.

He knew by the look on her face he'd said the right thing.

He also knew he'd be waiting a long time for her to get

over her fear of losing him and admit how she really felt.

He'd thought he had the patience of a saint. He'd thought he had all the time in the world to wait.

He'd thought she would one day come around.

But what if he were wrong?

Chapter Seven

LEAH WALKED THROUGH the foyer of Kindred Place, bypassing the welcoming interior without a second glance. As if in a fog, she headed straight toward the dining area where she set her bags down and arranged her baked goods on one of the tables.

A smile was plastered on her face, but she didn't really see the small group of people who called out to her.

She hadn't slept a wink last night. She couldn't.

The look on Grams' face haunted her. Every time she closed her eyes, she would see the disappointment in her grandmother's eyes, hear the betrayal in her voice as she finally understood just how bad the whole situation was.

So instead of sleeping, she baked.

Cinnamon buns.

Brownies.

Oatmeal chocolate chip cookies.

Lemon pound cake.

And even an apple crumble because that was Grams' favorite.

Baked and then booked her flight home.

Yes, she was running. So what? She'd been running when she came here and look how well that was turning out.

She grabbed a tray from the side and filled it with a plate of one of each of the goodies she'd made, along with two cups of coffee. It was the best she could do as a peace offering.

Leah wandered through the old Victorian house. Out of all the heritage buildings in Marietta, Kindred Place had always been her favorite. Her graduating class had taken their photo on the grand foyer stairs, she used to come trick-or-treating here every year, and even volunteered all throughout high school with the crafting group here every other afternoon—and by volunteering, it meant unwinding balls of yarn, refilling teacups, and attempting to knit her own socks, which turned out to be a massive failure.

She had a lot of memories in this old house.

Since it was early morning, things were on the quiet side. The low murmurs of TV shows hummed throughout the building, the occasional tap-tap of a cane as someone moved about, and the sporadic clumping of a pipe behind the walls were her only companions as she headed toward Grams' room.

Leah hit the tiny doorbell with her elbow while holding the tray in her hand. She could hear Grams moving around in her apartment and waited until the door opened.

"I come bearing apology gifts." Leah gave her grandmother a soft smile in greeting.

Grams leaned forward and looked over the plates on the tray. "You must have been up pretty early to make all this." She held the door open, inviting Leah to walk in.

"More like up all night." Leah walked through the cozy one-bedroom apartment and set the tray down on her grandmother's small dining table.

"The rest in the dining hall?" Grams pulled out a chair and sat. She took the offered coffee from Leah and sipped at it, a serene smile gracing her face that only another coffee-holic could understand.

"I think I saw a small herd congregate toward the table as I was leaving."

Grams puffed. "Of course they would. Kathy has been focusing on *clean eating* for the past month, and we're all dying for some sugar. Do you know she cleaned out all the cupboards of anything sweet and donated it to the local food bank?"

Kathy was the head cook and no, it didn't surprise Leah in the least.

"I remember you being all gung-ho for the healthy eating. What happened to living longer, being healthier, and all that other stuff you told me on the phone last month?"

Grams frowned before dipping her face into the mug of coffee. "That was before all the sugar withdrawals started happening. Twenty-five grumpy retirees in one room is never a good idea. She needs to bring that sugar back and fast. It's no wonder we're all congregating at Sage's for her chocolates and cocoa or at the pastry shop for pies and cakes. Wade's been sneaking in the odd cake here and there at night after Kathy has left the kitchen. Did I mention that?"

"Well, I could always do extra baking and leave it in Dylan's freezer for when I leave," Leah offered.

Grams sniffed. "That would be a good step in seeking forgiveness."

Ouch. Nothing like hitting where it hurts.

"I didn't mean any of the things I said," Leah protested, albeit a little weakly.

Grams knew it, too.

"If it wasn't how you felt, you never would have said it. Don't be blaming the alcohol for what's in your heart."

"But I don't feel that way. I love Marietta," Leah argued. "I mean, okay, I don't love it in the winter." She glanced down at the bright yellow rain boots she wore that did nothing, and she meant *nothing*, to keep her toes warm. "And no, I wouldn't want to move back here, but it doesn't mean I don't love this town. It's my home and it's where my family is. I would never…" She held her hand over her heart. "Never—"

"Just stop right there." Grams held up her hand palm out. "I'm not the one you need to convince. It's everyone else in this town that doesn't know you like I do. Once this gets out…" She shook her head with dismay. "The folks of Marietta will forgive a lot of things, Leah, but you might have gone too far with this one. Folks here…they've done a lot for you and your brother."

Leah stared down at the table, chagrined, knowing her grandmother was right. One hundred percent.

This small town had rallied around them after their parents had been killed by a drunk driver from a neighboring town. They supported the charity Leah worked for through multiple sponsorship drives and welcomed Dylan with open arms after he returned from college and started working at the local radio station.

"What can I do?" Leah asked. She'd been wracking her brain all night, trying to think of how to rectify the situation, but she was at a loss.

"You can stop hiding for one," Josie said. "What happened to you, girl? I don't like this defeatist persona you have on right now. Knock it off. Get out and about, talk to people, stop being shy and start being you. You can't will this to go away, so you might as well face it and apologize."

Leah's eyes grew wide at her grandmother's suggestion. "Ap-ap-apologize?" Admittedly, she had a hard time getting the word out.

"Yes. Apologize. Admit your mistake. Don't bother trying to offer an explanation. Just say you're sorry and show this town how wrong you were."

Leah attempted to pick at her piece of brownie, thankful she'd at least eaten a bowl of oatmeal before she'd come over. "Maybe that part won't come out," she said hopefully. So far, the media had been quiet about her remarks, only highlighting her broken heart and making fun of how she couldn't handle her drink. Nothing had been said yet about Marietta.

"And I'll go off sugar for the rest of my life," Grams said with heaps of sarcasm. "Get your head out of the clouds, girl. Own up to your mistakes before everyone finds out."

"But how?"

"You can't expect me to think of everything, can you? Have you talked to Wade about any of this?"

Leah scrunched up her nose at the mention of Wade's name.

Had she talked to him about this? No…and it took everything in her not to.

She wanted to.

She needed to.

It killed her not to.

Wade was her best friend. Until she'd went on the show, they shared everything.

Everything.

"He called last night," she whispered.

"Well, of course he did. You guys talk all the time." Grams tapped her fork over her plates of brownie, apple crumble, and cinnamon bun, as if trying to decide. "That doesn't answer my question though."

"Things aren't the same anymore."

Grams dropped her fork. "What? Why the hell—pardon

my language—not?"

Leah caught the *are-you-crazy* look on her grandmother's face, and she threw her hands up in the air with frustration.

"Don't you give me any of that 'he doesn't feel the same way anymore' nonsense either," Grams continued, ignoring Leah completely.

"He doesn't."

"That's nonsense." Grams dug into the apple crumble and took her first bite, the pure enjoyment on her face from the crisp, tart apples and sweet crumble eased a knot in Leah's heart she didn't realize was there.

"Girl, you've still got it." Grams took another bite before leaning backward with a contented sigh. "No one can make a crumble like you."

"I made an extra and placed it in Dylan's freezer so you'll have some after I leave." Leah had meant that to be a surprise. She'd even written a note labeled *For Grams only...hands off*, for Dylan in case he thought it was another treat for him. She'd made enough cinnamon buns to fill half his freezer, which should last him a few months at least.

"Of course you did. That's why you're my favorite granddaughter." Grams winked.

"I'm your only granddaughter." Leah rolled her eyes and took another bite of her brownie. She'd added a bit of caramel into the mix and liked how it tasted.

"When are you leaving?" Grams asked.

"Tomorrow." There was a bit of regret in Leah's voice,

and she didn't try to mask it.

"I see." Grams watched her, assessed her as if trying to read her mood, which, truth be told, shouldn't be too hard.

She was stressed.

When she was stressed, she baked. Just like—

"Your mother used to stress bake. You remind me so much of her. I would never tell my mother this, but my daughter out-baked her grandmother when it came to apple pies. Your crumble takes me back."

Leah leaned her elbows on the table. She loved whenever Grams talked about the past and especially about her mom.

"I remember the first time your mom made an apple pie all by herself. She was eight years old and wouldn't let my mom help her with the pie crust. We sat at that kitchen table, coffees in front of us, and just let her do her thing. We both thought the apple pie would fall apart or the crust would be soggy, but dang if she didn't hit it out of the ballpark. At eight years old." Grams wiped an errant tear that fell down her cheek and smiled.

"You miss her." Leah breathed the words, her heart aching from missing her mother.

"I miss them both." Grams gave her head a small shake. "There's another thing about your mother you need to remember. She was stubborn to a fault and never..." She leaned forward and grabbed a hold of Leah's hand, squeezing tight. "Never gave up on something she wanted."

The look she gave Leah...it said it all.

"It's not that easy, Grams." She needed her grandmother to understand.

"If there's one thing I've learned in all my years, it's that love is worth it. It's always worth it."

Love. Leah wanted to agree, she really did...but...she was too late. She'd made the mistake to think that Wade would always be there, that he would remain that one constant in her life and his love was something she could always fall back on. Instead of taking her time and not accepting what was already in her heart, she should have jumped in when he gave her the chance.

Leah tried not to live with regrets—*tried* being the optimum word there. But she had a feeling she would always regret giving up the one thing she needed the most in her life.

Wade.

Their relationship was different now, and she'd cried herself to sleep last night once she realized that. For some reason, she thought they could maintain the level of friendship they'd had for the past few years...but there was no coming back from blurting out *I love you* and not having it said back in return.

"It's not too late, Leah. Trust me. That boy...he's just waiting for you to open the door and let him in. So do it. Let him in."

Leah swallowed past the thick piece of brownie she'd just taken a bite of.

Let him in? Open the door? She'd tried that once, and he'd slammed it back closed by his silence. Could she do it again?

She wasn't too sure if she could handle having her heart broken all over again.

Chapter Eight

EVEN BEFORE STEPPING foot outside, Leah wound her scarf tighter around her neck. Snow was flying everywhere, and she could feel the chill in her bones even before she opened the door.

Good thing she was heading home soon. These rubber boots weren't doing much to keep her toes toasty warm, despite the thick wool socks and toe heaters she shoved inside before walking over this morning.

Head down, nose buried in her scarf, Leah headed down the walkway toward the sidewalk, not really paying attention to where she was going. All she wanted to do was head back to her brother's house, draw a warm bath, and then have a lovely little nap.

To say she was tired was an understatement.

Worn. Weary. Wiped.

It wasn't just the fact she hadn't slept. It was everything. The stress of what she'd done, of everything she'd gone through, it was like it all hit her at once. Her steps faltered and her foot slipped beneath her, sliding on ice. For one brief moment, she was free-falling backward until a strong grip stopped her.

"Oomph." The word rushed out from the impact.

"Careful there, Leah girl. Those rain boots aren't meant for ice, and I haven't put any sand down yet."

Wade, of all people, steadied her as she stood, his hand remaining on her arm until she stepped back.

"Thanks." She cleared her throat, unsure of what else to say.

"I figured that was your baking in the dining area this morning. No one else makes apple crumble like you." He looked her steady in the eyes. For one split second, Leah wanted to wrap herself in his embrace, tell him she was sorry, and…

And nothing. She pushed herself away from his touch and looked off into the distance.

"You must have been up all night baking that stuff. Either that or you were up at the crack of dawn."

Leah stole a glance toward Wade when she heard the teasing in his voice.

They both knew she wasn't a morning person.

"How about never went to bed?" The moment she said that, she realized her mistake. "I got your text last night but it was close to three in the morning when I saw it. I was going to respond today…"

"I came by last night."

"You did?" Stupid question. He obviously had or he

wouldn't have said it.

"Your bedroom light was on, so I threw some stones at it. Figured you either didn't hear or didn't want to see me." He looked away, as if afraid of what she'd say.

"Then why didn't you come to the front door like any normal human being?"

He shuffled his feet, stuck his hands in his pockets, and shrugged. "Figured you didn't want to see me," he mumbled. He stole a glance then.

She wanted to move closer, to take his hand and tell him the complete opposite.

Instead, she stayed in place and said nothing to contradict his words. It was easier that way.

She noticed he wasn't looking at her but rather at the scarf she wore around her neck. She fingered it, the wisps of a smile playing with her lips.

It was the ugliest scarf she owned, full of holes and knots, but when wrapped three times around her neck, it was the warmest.

It was also the most special one.

More so than the scarf Betsy had brought her back from Venice.

Wade had made this for her one Christmas, and it was the only scarf she wore now in the middle of winter.

"I can't believe you actually wear it." His voice broke as he reached for one of the ends that hung down toward her waist.

Did she mention it was also the longest scarf she owned, even when wrapped three times around her neck?

"I'm outside in the middle of a snowstorm; what else would I wear?"

He let go of the scarf and held his hand up to catch a few errant snowflakes. "I hardly call this a snowstorm."

Okay, okay, without the nasty wind, it was barely snowing. She'd give him that.

But still. Snow was snow and if it was swirling around her, it was a snowstorm.

"You'd never know you grew up here." He reached for a pail by his feet and started to sprinkle sand on the sidewalks.

"What's that supposed to mean?" She stepped out of his way and wiggled her toes to help keep them warm as she inadvertently stepped into a snow pile.

"Oh, come on. Like I have to spell it out, sun girl." He kept his gaze on the task at hand, not looking at her.

She frowned. "What's wrong with preferring the sun over the snow?" She wrapped her arms around herself and shivered.

Wade chuckled, and the sound of his laugh was like stepping into a hot bath. It was the best feeling in the world on a cold winter's day.

"Why are you laughing at me?" She tried pretending she was bothered when it was really the one sound she loved to hear the most.

"What happened to the girl who built snowmen, skied

along the trails, and snowshoed all over the countryside? The one who swore she felt more alive living outside than anywhere else?"

"I'm still that same girl."

"Are you?"

"Of course I am." He thought she'd changed? She didn't like that. "I just prefer the sun, the sand, and the surf rather than the snow and being cold. So very, very cold." She rubbed her hands together and wished she'd chosen warmer mitts rather than the thin leather ones she'd found in her room.

Wade set the bucket in his hands down, took her hands, and peeled off the thin pieces of leather.

"What..." It didn't take long for her to understand what he was doing. He sandwiched her cold digits between his. He was like a heat lamp, and she instantly felt the warmth seep into her skin.

"Do you ever get cold?" She looked up at him and was swept away at the look on his face.

It was as if standing here, with her, warming her up, was all he wanted to do. Like there was nothing else in the world but them in this moment.

"You've been away too long, is all." His husky voice was doing something to her, something she didn't want to admit. Something that was close to making her remember how she felt about him...and how much it hurt to have him turn from her.

She pulled her hands away and stuffed them in her pockets.

"Yeah, well…I'm leaving soon, anyway." She swallowed hard and refused to look at him, not wanting to see if there was a look of relief or disappointment on his face.

She didn't think she could handle either, truth be told.

"I, ah…I should go." Leah stomped her feet on the ground to dislodge the snow on her boots and turned from him.

She'd taken five steps. Five steps away from him before he called out.

"What are you doing this afternoon?"

She half turned. "Right now, my only plan is to sleep." She pulled the scarf up over her mouth and nose.

"Well, Sleeping Beauty, once you get that rest, dress warm and be ready at four o'clock."

Leah scrunched the scarf down to her chin and gave him a measured look. She didn't quite like the glint in his eyes or the way his chin dimple deepened as he barely contained his laughter.

She knew he wanted to laugh. She could see it, and she knew him.

He had something up his sleeve.

"What's happening at four o'clock?" she asked.

The man who wore only a thick wool sweater and scarf shrugged his shoulders before giving her the shooing gesture.

"You'll see. Now go, get warmed up and sleep." He

picked up the pail and continued to sprinkle the sand.

Leah shook her head and continued toward home. He wanted her to dress warmly? He'd better not be taking her out into the bush to track deer or something crazy like that. Oh, who was she kidding? That was probably exactly what he had up his sleeve.

No way. There was no way she was traipsing out into the snow. Not today. Not tomorrow, not any time soon.

If she had proper clothing…maybe. Wade was right— once upon a time, she loved being outside in the cold. She would come home to Marietta excited about the adventures Wade would take her on into the bush.

When she'd seen his text early this morning, and by early, she hadn't lied; it had been around three in the morning when she stumbled her way up to her room for a change of clothes after soaking the sleeves of her arms in the sink. Her heart sank to realize what she'd missed.

She'd been tempted to text him back but knew he slept with his phone on the charger beside him, and the last thing she wanted was to wake him up.

She should have texted him this morning, though. She shouldn't have ignored him.

It didn't take long to reach Dylan's front porch. She looked back to see if she could still see Wade and, sure enough, he stood on the sidewalk, facing her. Probably watching to make sure she made it home okay.

She lifted her hand in a wave. Even though she couldn't

see the smile on his face, she felt it and it warmed her to the tip of her toes.

She sagged against the door after closing it behind her. Why had she waited so long? Why hadn't she seen what was right in front of her?

That man out there—that man was the best thing in her life and she'd taken him for granted.

She didn't blame him for not waiting for her, even though he'd promised he would.

She blamed herself.

AFTER SEVERAL BLISSFUL hours of sleep, Leah pushed the blankets off and rolled out of bed. She stood at the window, curtains opened wide. Instead of a flurry of swirling snow, everything was bright, beautiful, and the snow even sparkled like diamonds.

Donning a warm sweater and her Mukluks, Leah headed into the kitchen where she found a note from her big brother. The same big brother who had taken one look at her earlier and helped tuck her into bed, even heating up one of the throw blankets she'd been using earlier and placing it at her feet.

Go grab a hot cocoa from Copper Mnt Chocolates. I paid for it already. Sage wants to chat.

Good luck.

Any good mood Leah had upon waking quickly evaporated.

Sage wanted to chat? That didn't sound good. In fact, it sounded ominous.

He should have left out the last two sentences. She would gladly have made her way to Sage's shop for a hot cocoa.

She unplugged her phone from the wall charger where she'd left it earlier and saw the exact same message via text.

This thing with Sage, she texted back. *When you say chat, do you mean a good, let's-catch-up kind of chat or…*

Ten seconds, or what seemed like an eternity later, Dylan finally replied.

I didn't think to ask. Heading into work. See you tonight.

Didn't think to ask? What kind of man didn't think to ask when a woman said she wanted to chat?

"Karma, let's be friends today, okay? Pretty please?" She'd had enough of bad luck and unpleasant experiences come her way the past month; it was time for something good to happen in her life.

The first thing on her to-do list tomorrow after flying home was to contact the office at KIND to see if they could send her on a road trip or something.

While she got ready to head down to the chocolate shop, Leah sent her boss an email, asking exactly that. And if they could talk about a time frame for her to come back to work. The media frenzy was bound to die down. Hopefully by now, something else had cropped up on the show for the sharks to circle around.

Maybe that was why Betsy had been calling.

On that note...

"Oh. My. God. Leah, you actually called me back," Betsy answered on the first ring. "I was starting to think you were ignoring me, weren't you?"

It was great to hear Betsy's cheerful, carefree, and chipper voice even though technically she was still mad at her.

"I wasn't ignoring you." Well...maybe a little. It wasn't so much as ignoring as not being ready to talk to her. There was a difference.

"Really? You've been so busy hiding in that backwater little town of yours that you can't spare a few minutes for your BFF?"

"That wasn't nice. We've texted." Leah sank down in a chair. She heard the hurt in Betsy's voice and had a little twinge of guilt. She should have called back sooner.

"Texting is not the same and you know it. Doesn't feel nice being ignored, I'll say that much. You're not still mad at me, are you?"

Leah could picture the pout on her friend's face. "Betsy, it hasn't exactly been all fun and games, you know. I couldn't go home because of the reporters, the amount of messages on my phone would stress even you out, and..."

"I ruined your life, I know. I feel horrible. I really do."

Leah couldn't tell if there was actual sincerity in Betsy's voice or if she realized how trite she sounded right then.

"I want to make it up to you," Betsy gushed.

"How?" What could her friend do to make the nightmare of her life any better? Send her to a spa for the day? Order one of those fancy baskets Betsy basically got for free thanks to the marketing from *Charmed*? That wasn't Leah's world, it was Betsy's. Those were things Betsy would love, not Leah.

She just wanted to be left alone.

"Before you say anything, just hear me out, okay? I need you to promise."

Leah snorted. "I'm not promising you anything. I've learned my lesson." Betsy had used the same sentences last time and Leah had blindly promised, but not just to hear her out. If she remembered correctly, she said something along the lines of *I don't need to promise; you know I'm your girl if you are in a bind.*

Well, she was no longer that girl, that was for sure.

"Ouch."

"Can you blame me?" Leah asked.

There was silence on the other end of the phone before Betsy grumbled incoherently before she gave her typical *oh-well-this-is-me* giggle.

"Of course I don't blame you, silly. That's why I want to make it up. I have the best idea ever. It's going to make right all my wrongs, I promise."

"No more promises, please." Leah could write a book based on all the promises Betsy had made throughout the years and broke.

"Fine, fine. Just hear me out, okay? I've thought up the

best idea and even got the approval from my boss, which, as you know, is a miracle of itself. I sold it as helping boost ratings. Everyone loves a happy-ever-after story and—"

"No." No matter what Betsy was about to suggest, her answer was simple.

No. Hell no. Not-in-this-world no.

"But...come on, Leah. Just hear me out, please."

Betsy could beg, plead, tempt, and promise the world, but the answer would still be no.

"This will be good for you. It'll solve everything, I prom...oops." Betsy giggled while Leah gritted her teeth. "Let me bring up a team to your little town and do a focus story. On you, on the town, and on your romance with Wade. We'll sell it as *Lonely Leah Finds Love*, and everything that happened gets erased. No more drinking issues, no more broken hearts, and you get back in the good graces after the things you said about Marietta. It's a win-win for everyone. In fact, if you read the gossip papers tomorrow, you'll see that we took care of the whole alcohol thing." Betsy tripped over her words in her rush to get them out before Leah could stop her. It was like watching a runaway dog, knowing there was nothing to do but stand there and trust the silly thing came home...eventually.

Except, this was no dog and there was no hope for return.

"What do you mean, you took care of the whole alcohol thing?" Why did she have a feeling she was about to be skewered with the dull edge of a spoon?

"We found out who switched your glasses, that's all." Betsy's voice was chipper. Too chipper. "Someone made an anonymous confession, leaked it to the right source, and it's about to be plastered all over the news."

"Who?" Leah's mind raced in circles as she tried to remember the happenings of that day. It was very possible her glasses had been switched, but by who?

"One of the girls. Don't worry about it. We've taken care of it." There was a measure of satisfaction in those words, along with a measure of pride.

"What did you do?" Betsy had told her, multiple times, that to keep a job with *Charmed*, you had to be cutthroat and willing to cross a few lines.

She always warned Betsy there were a few lines that should never be crossed.

"I promised you I'd take care of it, and I did. Just say thank you and agree that me coming to Marietta is a brilliant idea."

Brilliant idea? No way.

"I'm leaving in the morning, so don't bother. It'd be a waste of a trip."

"But..." Betsy inhaled, the sound reminding Leah of a whistle. "If you weren't leaving in the morning, you'd do it? That's awesome! I'll cover the cost of you flying home afterward, too, so don't worry about that. Send the receipt for the cancelled flight to me, and I'll get you reimbursed.

Thankyou-thankyou-thankyou."

"Whoa, slow down, that's not what I said at all." Leah knew when she was about to get steamrolled by the Betsy train, and this was one of those times. "No. I said no, and I really mean it. I love you, but I'm out. No more favors. No more last-minute miracles. I don't know if I have a job because of your show, my reputation is ruined, and Grams is not all that thrilled with the comments I made." Leah leaned her head back against the wall and closed her eyes. "No, Betsy. I just want to go home."

"I know I made a mess of things. Please, let me make it up to you."

She loved Betsy. She really did. But…

"Unless you can turn back time, I think you've done more than enough." She rubbed the kink in the back of her neck. If it weren't for seeing Wade again this afternoon, she'd wish this day over.

She wasn't sure what he had in store for them, but she was intrigued. And maybe, just maybe, they could talk about the phone call and his response and…

"Don't come home. Please? Give me three days. That's all I ask. Three days to make amends. You won't even know we're there. Well…" She caught herself. "You will but I promise it won't be a bad experience. Everyone has promised to be on their best behavior and the only focus we have is rebuilding what we torn apart."

Was Betsy serious right now? Did she not hear her say

no? Leah couldn't get over the gall Betsy had. Shouldn't surprise her though. Betsy did work in reality television, and she was quite good at her job.

"Betsy, for the last time, no. Drop it okay?" Just like she was ready to drop this conversation.

"Think about it, please? The producers want to make it up to you. I want to make it up to you. Please, please, just think about it. That's all I ask," Betsy begged.

There was a small part of Leah that liked having Betsy beg, truth be told.

But there was a larger part that was ready for a break. From Betsy. From the mess and chaos that came from having Betsy in her life.

Of the many lessons she'd learned from this whole experience, it was that.

No more chaos. No more messiness. She was ready to focus on her career, living with more peace in her life, and maybe, one day, finding love.

If she could get over Wade.

Which she doubted would ever happen.

Chapter Nine

THE MOMENT LEAH opened the door to Copper Mountain Chocolates, she was ready for that cocoa and for whatever else Sage was cooking up for the day.

When she opened the door, there was a line at the counter but only one table occupied.

Leah waited her turn, somewhat patiently, while pursuing the display in search of a treat to nibble on. She didn't notice that the line in front of her disappeared and she was the only customer left in the store.

"Are you going to stand there all day and drool over the chocolates or just eat one?" Sage set a mug of her cocoa down on the counter and laughed at her.

"Sorry." Leah gave her head a shake. "I'm a little out of it today."

"No kidding. Dylan mentioned you stayed up all night baking. Where's my cinnamon bun, huh?"

Leah's eyes widened. "Oh, gosh, I'm sorry. I…"

Sage held up her hand, smile wide across her face. "I'm only teasing. Dylan brought one in already."

Leah reached for her cocoa and breathed in deep. "I basically filled his freezer with baking so if you're wanting more, just say the word." God, she loved the smell of this cocoa. She had no idea what Sage put into it. It was hands down the best she'd ever tried.

"Come and meet my niece, Portia. She's been working here since October, and we could use a break after stamping all these foils for our gold coins." Sage grabbed a tray with two cups and a small plate of treats and led the way to the table in the corner where Portia sat.

"What are the coins for?" Leah asked as she sat and looked at the stack of foil sheets on the extra chair.

"The St. Paddy's Day hunt. We hide them all throughout the town. It's pretty fun, actually. I'm trying something different this year, though." Sage nodded toward the plate she'd set in the middle of the table.

The chocolates on the plate were round, all the same size and thickness, but that was about all that was similar to them. They were all different flavors, from what Leah could surmise.

"Oh, different coins," Leah said. "I like it."

Sage broke a chocolate circle into pieces, passing each of them one to taste.

"Different chocolates with different colored foils. Normally, we only do one color—gold—but Portia came up with the idea, and well...why not?"

Leah glanced over at Portia who blushed.

"I think it's perfect. Come on." Leah reached for another piece of coconut milk chocolate. "Who doesn't love this stuff anyway, right?"

"What are you going to do when you move back to California and don't have your brother bringing home my chocolates or hot cocoa?" Sage leaned back in her chair and studied Leah.

She squirmed in her chair a little, feeling very uncomfortable. Not from the question but from the look her old friend gave her.

"Come back home more often?" Leah assumed that was the correct answer. From the satisfied grin on Sage's face, it indeed was.

"That might be a good thing, unless you want people believing the nonsense written about you in the papers."

Leah's hand froze as she reached for her mug. To have someone else talk about it—someone not in her family...the fist-sized ball of panic locked in place within her grew.

"The nonsense?" she squeaked.

"Yes, the nonsense." Sage frowned. "You remember...where you called Marietta a backwater town in the middle of nowhere surrounded by ranches and cowboys?" Sage looked her straight in the eye, leaving Leah wishing she were anywhere but here. "That you couldn't wait to leave and spread your wings, to discover there was more to life than what our small town has to offer," she continued.

Portia coughed discreetly while Leah squirmed even

more.

"Sage…" Leah wanted her friend to understand. It was more than a want. It was a need. She needed Sage to understand, just like she needed her town to understand that she never meant those words…not like that.

"Was it worth it?"

Leah shook her head. "It was the biggest mistake of my life." Her phone rang, and she pulled it out of her jacket to give it a quick look.

Betsy. Leah shook her head. Seriously, could the girl not take no for an answer?

"Is it important?" Sage asked before Leah could decide whether she wanted to answer it or not.

Her conversation with Josie this morning played through her mind. She would need to show the people of Marietta that they were important to her, and while she had no idea how to do that…she knew it would take little steps.

Like this one.

She hit the ignore button, shut off the volume, and stashed the phone back in her coat pocket.

"No, it's not important." Not as important as being here, in the present, with her friend. She wasn't going to be in Marietta much longer, but for the time she was here, she would make it count.

"Sage, this is my home. No matter what happens to me, this…" She glanced out the front window and thought of what Marietta really meant to her.

It was home. It was safe. It was…heartache and comfort and growth and security and…

"This is where you run to lick your wounds."

Leah nodded. "I was wrong. I…that show took advantage of me, and I'd let my walls down. I trusted someone I shouldn't have, and it cost me in the end."

"So it's all true?" Sage took a sip of her cocoa and watched her over the brim of her cup.

Leah wrinkled her nose. "I don't think it's all true. They embellish a lot." She let out a very long sigh. *"Charmed* isn't…exactly what I thought it would be. It's…crazier than what you see on television. There's so much that happens behind the scenes, it's almost scary."

"Did you get the bracelet?" Portia paused in stamping the foil and gave Leah her full attention.

"Portia…"

"No, it's okay," Leah reassured Sage. "I did get a bracelet, with tiny charms. It's actually really pretty. I had to sign a contract that I wouldn't sell it or the charms for at least two years, though."

"Why would you want to sell it?" Portia asked. "I'd keep that forever as a reminder of the experience."

Leah snorted. "If the experience was a good one, sure."

"What do you mean?"

Leah pursed her lips. She wasn't allowed to talk about it. Non-disclosure agreement and all that stuff. She'd tell those closest to her, but everyone else…she needed to figure out what to say and how to say it.

"Things aren't always how they appear on the show is what I think she means, right?" Sage offered on Leah's behalf.

Leah nodded, thankful for Sage stepping in.

"So, what's it like? The mansions always look amazing and—" Portia leaned forward, completely intent on finding more about what the hit reality television show was really like.

"It looks like a fairy tale, right?" Leah said. She hated to destroy Portia's obvious love for the show. "Not all fairy tales have happy endings, at least, not the original ones. *Charmed* is whatever you want it to be. A fairy tale, a nightmare…it's basically a *choose your own adventure* but shared with millions of other people."

Portia seemed to take that in. She leaned back and placed her hand on her expanding belly, rubbing it gently as she did so, and gave her a thoughtful nod. "Doesn't sound like the fairy tale I'd want."

It took Leah a moment to respond; she was transfixed by Portia's pregnancy. She cast a glance toward Portia's hands and noticed the absence of a wedding ring.

"Me neither," Leah finally said. Guess she wasn't the only one disappointed by fairy tales. She wasn't going to prod, but she couldn't help but be curious as to Portia's story—why she was here in Marietta, pregnant and working for Sage.

"But your friend works for the show, right?" Sage asked.

Leah swirled the cocoa in her mug around a little, watching as the whipped cream dissolved into the chocolate gold and took a sip before she nodded. "Right. I was on there to do her a favor. She had a last-minute cancellation, and she would have been fired if she didn't find a replacement."

"Fired? On *Charmed*? They wouldn't do that." Portia was taken back.

Leah chuckled. "Oh honey, in the land of reality television, there are no second chances. It's a sharks' world, and I should have known better."

She did know better. It was why she'd called Dylan for advice. She couldn't call Wade for many reasons, one of them being he was on a guided hike in the woods. Another being it would have been extremely uncomfortable given her proclamation of love and his avoidance of that declaration.

Portia reached across, placing her hand on Leah's arm for a second. "I'm so sorry. It sounds like it was anything but a fairy tale."

"So, the comments…" Sage brought the subject back around.

"Would you believe that fruit-flavored dessert wine mixed with soda doesn't taste like alcohol? Especially when you're forced to sit in the hot sun all day with very little food to eat?"

Sage's eyes grew rounder than the chocolate coins on the table.

"You don't drink," she said.

The breath Leah let out hurt. It came from the bottom of her soul and was full of wishes and regrets. "They knew that, too. I guess someone overheard me talking with Betsy about how I was only supposed to be there the first night, and then they decided to take a very boring day and make it into something more show-worthy. They wanted explosive and that's exactly what happened." She half turned in her seat, facing Sage directly.

"I am so sorry for everything I said. I was heartbroken and going on that show wasn't the way to deal with it. I love Marietta. It will always be my home, and it was wrong of me to say otherwise."

Sage looked at her, searching her gaze as if to read the truth in her eyes.

Leah had never been more honest.

"I believe you," Sage finally said.

Leah's whole body sagged with relief.

"I hate to tell you this though, Leah, but…" Sage winced as if she knew the words she was about to say would hurt.

She didn't need to say them though.

"But I have a lot of work ahead of me, don't I?" If Sage read about what she'd said in the papers, then it was almost guaranteed everyone else in Marietta had, too.

"Josie says I need to stop hiding and get out there, talk to everyone before I leave, which happens to be tomorrow morning." Leah glanced at her watch and realized it was already after four o'clock. She was late.

"If I can give you a piece of advice? Cancel your flight and stay for another week, at least. Otherwise, you look really guilty. It will only back up everything the media has been saying—whether it's true or not."

Leah startled. "That's exactly what Betsy suggested."

"Betsy's the producer friend? And she wants you to stay?" Sage frowned.

"She wants to bring a production crew up here for a day or two to film me, this town...something about *Lonely Leah Finds Love*, except..." Her throat suddenly became very dry, like the air in Arizona on a hot summer day dry, and she couldn't get the words out.

"That might be a good idea. We have our St. Paddy's scavenger hunt happening. It would get some coverage, I'm sure. Might be good for the town, you know?" Sage stood and gathered all the cups and plates of now-empty chocolate pieces onto the tray she'd set to the side. "What harm could it do?"

Leah choked on the last bit of cocoa she'd taken a sip. What harm? What harm?

"Trust me, you don't want them here." A brief snapshot of the chaos *Charmed* would bring to Marietta was enough to give Leah a headache. "Sure, great marketing for Marietta and for you and your chocolates, but they want to focus it on *Lonely Leah Finds Love*." She rolled her eyes. "Little too late for that."

"Why's that?" Sage paused with the tray in hand.

Oops. She hadn't meant to say that out loud.

"I don't mean to pry, but what's going on with you and Wade?" Sage placed the tray over on the counter and came back to the table, hand on hip and looking like she had plenty on her mind when it came to her and Wade.

Everyone assumed a lot about them. They assumed they would one day end up together, that the love and friendship between them would always be there.

Heck, even she'd assumed that.

"Nothing," Leah finally admitted. "Absolutely nothing is going on, and that's the problem."

"Are you sure about that?" Portia, who had sat there quiet as a ladybug on a leaf, spoke up.

"I'm very sure." One day it wouldn't hurt to admit that, right?

Sage's hand rested on Leah's shoulder. She squeezed lightly.

"Are you sure you're leaving tomorrow?" Sage asked.

Leah nodded and was caught off guard by the hug she received from her old friend.

She wasn't prepared at the tears that gathered in her own eyes as she hugged Sage back.

Until now she hadn't realized just how much she'd missed her.

"If you must leave tomorrow, don't be a stranger, okay? Come back soon and let's keep in touch. You've got my number. Call me some time," Sage said.

"It's a date." She might not be able to right all the wrongs in her life, but she could take care of this one. She needed friends. Friends who loved her for her, not for what she did for them. Friends who weren't toxic…like the ones she had in California.

Truth be told, it might be harder to leave Marietta than she'd thought it would be.

Chapter Ten

WADE STEPPED BACK and looked at what he'd built with satisfaction.

That was a darn good snowman if he did say so himself.

He had no idea where Leah was, but he wasn't leaving until he saw her. If it meant he had to fill the front yard with snowmen, then that was exactly what he would do.

He was in the middle of rolling the middle section of his second snowman when he had a niggling feeling that he was being watched.

As carefully as possible, Wade filled the palm of his gloves with snow and patted it into a snowball.

He sure hoped he wasn't about to regret this. He tossed the snowball over his shoulder and heard the satisfying *oomph* from Leah.

Yes! Wade gave a small fist pump before he turned around with an innocent look on his face. He hoped.

"How did you know it was me?" Leah brushed off the snow from her coat. "What if it'd been Grams?"

"She would know better than to stand behind me." He

knelt and grabbed more snow, lobbing it at her before she had the chance to move.

She made it so easy.

"No fair." She ran toward his truck, hiding behind it but not fast enough.

He hit her in the back. He had to admit, he was enjoying this.

He could see her fighting against the need to protest and run into the house—and the desire to hit him square in the face with a snowball of her own.

She had quite the arm, so he wouldn't put it past her.

He caught her trying to edge closer to the front door, but there was no way he was letting that happen. Bending down so she couldn't see him thanks to the truck she hid behind, he made his way toward to the front of it. He listened to the crunch of her feet on the snow and crouched.

The moment she made a run for it, he jumped out and grabbed her, enveloping her in a big bear hug.

A rush of laughter escaped from her, her face lighting up as he twirled her around.

Wade's heart swelled with happiness. This was what he'd been missing. Her laughter. Her smile. The feel of her in his arms. He breathed it all in, unsure of how long it would last.

"You don't play fair," she finally said when she caught her breath.

"Didn't know I needed to." Wade winked as he casually brushed the snow off her shoulders. He tried to hide his smile as he noticed her wearing the scarf he'd made her for Christmas.

"What kind of boots are you wearing?" He stared at the bright yellow rain boots on her feet. Rain boots. What in her right mind would make her wear those? "You've been in California too long. Forget it snows here in March still?" He liked teasing her, enjoyed that smile that grew on her face, the way her eyes sparkled just before she laughed.

"My idiot of a brother got rid of all my snow gear apparently. It's why I'm wearing this oversized coat." She pulled at the hem of her jacket and then kicked her feet. "These boots are horrible. If I'd known he was going to get rid of my Merrell's, I'd have taken them with me to California. Those were the best boots I've ever worn." The frown on her face told him a lot more than she probably wanted to.

She did miss the snow. It was part of her—this beautiful country—and as much as she pretended to be a sun baby now, being a country girl was who she was. That would never change.

"Couldn't you just order new ones online?"

She shook her head. "Why bother? Besides, my brother promised the weather was supposed to turn and all this snow was to melt." She hid her face from him, so he moved to step directly into her line of sight.

"You should know your brother is rarely right, especially when it comes to snow, rain, or anything that drops from the sky. Sunny days…he tends to get those more right than wrong."

He could see she was about to argue, to defend her brother, which was really cute, but she didn't. It surprised him.

"You're trying to pick a fight with me, aren't you?" she said instead.

He shrugged. His goal was to remind her of what they had together, of why she belonged here…so any emotional response was welcomed.

"Why?" Hands on hips, she got in his face and looked up.

"Cause you've said nothing about my snowman."

"Your…snowman?" She looked behind him with a confused expression.

"You're dissin' my snowman?"

"Dissin'?" The look Leah gave him was priceless.

"The last tour group taught me some new slang."

Leah laughed. Actually laughed at him.

"What?"

She headed toward her front door, and he felt a moment of panic that she was leaving him.

"Wade, you're showing your age. I don't think anyone has used *dissin'* in years."

"Where are you going?" He rushed to the front steps, one foot on the bottom one, ready to follow her if needed. He had a date planned with her, and there was no way he was letting her get out of it.

"That snowman of yours needs a little help," she said before entering the house and closing the door behind her.

Well, all righty then.

Wade looked at his snowman and thought it looked fine, but hey, if she wanted to dress it up, then he wasn't about to stop her.

While he waited for her, he went back to the ball he'd been rolling for the second snowman.

He'd set the head on top just as she opened the door, her arms heavy with...stuff.

"I leave for a few minutes and now there's two?" She relinquished a bit of her load into his hands.

"One for me and one for you."

He wondered if she remembered the times they would build snowmen when they were younger. The contests they'd have to see who could build the biggest one or the most within a certain time frame. Wade wondered if she ever remembered the fun they had.

"I don't ever remember agreeing to build a snowman." She took one of the carrots she'd brought out and stuck it on one of the faces.

"Good thing you didn't build one, I guess." Wade took the other carrot and repeated her action.

Within a few moments, their snowmen were all decorated.

"It's been a while since I've decorated one of these. We kind of don't get snow back home." Leah's cheeks were a cozy red.

"You are home," Wade reminded her. He didn't like hearing her talk about California like that. This would always be where she belonged.

"You know what I mean." She gave him a sideways glance, but he pretended to not see it.

"I don't, actually. I don't think anyone else here would either." He reached for her hand and pulled her toward the truck. "Come on; it's time to go."

She pulled back. "Time to go? Go where?"

He watched as her hand pulled out of his. It felt like she was cutting herself from him, creating even more of a distance, and he wasn't about to let that happen.

He opened the passenger door of his truck and waited for Leah to hop in.

She just stood there, arms crossed, looking like a petulant little girl.

He scratched the back of his neck. What was it going to take to break through that wall she was building around herself? He could see it. Josie could see it. Heck, Sage could see it. Why couldn't she?

"Hop in the truck, Leah. It's not like I'm kidnapping you or anything. Would you trust me a little, please?"

"Not till you tell me where we're going."

Wade pulled out a pair of skates and held them up for her to see. "We're going ice skating, okay? Simple ice skating." He shook his head and dropped the skates. "Seems you need help remembering what home truly means."

"Oh, really?" Her brow arched and that fire he knew and loved flared in her eyes. "And you aim to help with that?" The old country drawl, the one that made her voice smooth as whipped butter, came back. She only spoke like that when she was angry.

He didn't mind an angry Leah. He'd much rather that emotion than her being all cold on him.

"That's what best friends are for, aren't they?" As if he needed to remind her of that.

He didn't know what was with her, didn't get why she seemed to be hiding from him, but it was one more thing to add to his recent list of dislikes.

"Some days I swear this best-friends business is a load of horse manure," she mumbled before climbing into his truck.

Wade tried really hard not to react to that. It sounded to him like she wasn't enjoying the status quo they'd held for so many years.

Was it possible those things he'd read about, her drunken confessions on the show *Charmed*, were actually real?

Could she really love him?

Chapter Eleven

LEAH COULDN'T KEEP up the pretense of being grumpy for long.

It didn't help that Wade stopped at Sage's for more hot chocolate.

Or that he'd thought ahead and brought hand warmers to go inside her mitts once at the lake.

Or that he'd even brought some thicker wool socks for her to wear.

Or that he'd somehow managed to find skates for her to use.

Not to mention the way he'd smile when he thought she wasn't looking, or how his dimple would deepen as he struggled to hide said smile when looking her way.

She'd given up pretending to be in a bad mood and decided to just enjoy the day. She knew there wouldn't be many more like this one—days spent with Wade having fun. In fact, it was probably the last time they'd spend an afternoon together in a long time.

Leah's breath caught as Wade pulled up to Miracle Lake

where they'd be skating. There was a legend about this lake—about how someone had fallen through the ice and drowned only to be revived and go on to live a very long life. She remembered her mom warning her when she was younger about the dangers of ice and what to look for when skating on it.

The white snow around them glistened as the sun's rays shone down.

Diamonds sparkled on the snow as Leah followed Wade along the pathway.

Ever since the wind had lifted earlier, the day turned out beautiful and full of promise. Just like her brother had predicted. She wasn't the only one to think so either. The area surrounding the outdoor ice rink was full of town people out enjoying the weather.

A group of children off to the side were busy building snowmen while their mothers stood to the side and talked with each other. Leah tightened her grip on her cup and raised a hand in greeting. She recognized a few of the faces, but she wasn't sure if what she saw was welcoming smiles or gossiping grins.

Her steps faltered as the temptation to turn around and head back to Wade's truck grew strong. He must have sensed it because when he turned, he reached out for her and placed his arm around her waist.

"Come on, no backing out now. Let's see if you still re-member how to slide around on ice," he said gently.

Leah breathed in deep. Grams told her she'd have to make amends. Face the storm of gossip. Running back to Dylan's place wouldn't be doing that.

"They have ice rinks in California, I'll have you know." Leah didn't even bother to keep the sarcasm from her voice.

"Do they now? Well, I guess we'll see if you're still worthy of your title, Twinkle Toes." He gave a very saucy wink before leading her to the benches around the lake.

She knew what he was doing and appreciated it more than he could understand.

With her head down, Leah laced up the skates Wade had brought, sipped on the last bit of her cocoa, and waited for him to lead her out onto the ice.

There was no way she was going on there without him. Not with the way people were watching her and whispering amongst themselves.

They'd either all seen the magazine articles or they'd heard about them. Either way, it was time to face the music, so to speak.

"Are you ready?" Wade's gentle voice reminded her she wasn't in this alone.

"Do I have much of a choice?" she asked. Even though they hadn't talked about this...he got it. He understood. Truthfully, she shouldn't be surprised.

"You always have a choice." He looked around before giving her his hand. "The decision is up to you on what you choose."

"What are my options?" She placed her hand in his and let him help her stand.

"Way I see it, you can do one of two things. Forget what's going on around you and just enjoy the day or assume all the whispering is about you and get all stressed." He led the way toward the ice. "Personally, I vote for enjoying the day. Your brother says tomorrow is supposed to be sunny with no chance of snow so you know what that means."

Once on the ice, he skated backward, a large and obnoxious grin on his face.

"It means it'll be a sunny day with no chance of snow." Her brother was almost always wrong, and yet she'd stick up for him every time.

"Not if you want to go on that trip, it won't be." He wiggled his brows before turning and skating ahead of her.

She hurried to catch up, enjoying the way it felt to glide across the ice. This was how she learned to skate—on Marietta's frozen lake, where the ice was uneven and red pylons indicated areas of thinner ice. Not like the ice in California that was man-made smooth.

"I have a feeling you've already won enough to pay for that trip," she said once she finally caught up to him.

"Maybe," he said with a smile and a shrug. He'd slowed down so they could skate side by side. When he reached for her hand, she was more than happy to place it in his.

Enjoy the day. That was what she chose to do.

"Oh, look at you two," a voice gushed behind them.

"Holding hands like a regular couple. It's about time, too. Guess you're no longer Lonely Leah, isn't that right?"

Leah went to pull her hand from Wade's, but he held on tight as they slowed down to talk to the person behind them.

Make that *people* behind them.

Jay and Jen Patterson were there, wide smiles on their faces along with two children, Justin and Jasmine.

"Hey there, guys. Great day for skating, isn't it?" Wade greeted them with warmth.

Leah plastered a smile on her face, standing there awkwardly. Why hadn't she thought of some snappy responses to this name she'd been given?

"Why on earth would they call you Lonely Leah to begin with? All they had to do was ask anyone here in Marietta and we could have told them about you two." Jen gave what Leah knew to be a genuine smile, but it only made Leah want to turn and run as fast as she could out of there. Or rather, skate.

Leah wrapped her arms around herself.

Wade broke the silence. "Sage..." He cleared his throat. "She, uh, wanted me to let everyone here know that she has free cookies to go with her cocoa if you stop by." He looked down at Leah. "I snagged some for later. Don't worry."

She meant to laugh, but the sound came out more like a snort. "I wasn't worried. But I think you should do a couple of laps around before you eat any cookies."

Wade wrapped her arm through his, nodding to the other couple in acknowledgement. "True enough."

They skated ahead, and Leah didn't speak until she knew they wouldn't be overheard.

"I hate that name," she mumbled.

"It's only a name. Don't let it bother you." He patted her hand before he pushed himself forward, turned, and skated backward.

"Show off."

He gave her a thumbs-up, and then wiggled his fingers in a come-and-get-it move.

Her brow arched.

So did his.

She sighed and put some speed into her movement until she caught up to him and skated around him.

"There she is. Miss Twinkle Toes herself." He held out his hand and pulled her alongside of him so that they skated next to one another.

Wade never let go of her hand. To be honest, she didn't want him to. There were moments when he would look at her and she'd swear he was going to pull her into his arms...except, he didn't. He'd place a little bit of distance between them, a smile on his face, and pretend the ribbons of passion that continued to pull at them didn't exist.

She could feel them. Every time they touched, there was a spark. Every time their gazes connected, there was a sense of *rightness*.

To say she was frustrated was an understatement.

To admit she was more than a little bit confused…well, truth be told, she was more than just a little confused.

This was going to be the last day she spent with him, the last day of *this* between them before she went back home, so why in-all-that-was-holy-and-right did she want to do anything *but* leave?

She wanted to stay.

She wanted to tell him how she felt.

She wanted to pull him close and kiss him, for once, just to know what it would be like to taste him.

Except she couldn't and wouldn't and no-way-in-h-e-double-hockey-sticks could she make that kind of first move.

"Everything okay?" Wade pulled her close, just like she'd been imagining, and looked deep into her eyes. They'd slowed down, but continued to move forward, with him skating backward, facing her.

"Just…wishing…" Her gaze drifted to his lips. The sound of his chuckle had her dragging her eyes from those irresistible lips to his eyes, which danced with glee.

"Anything I can help with?" His smile deepened as he pulled her even closer.

It would be so easy just to lean forward and lift herself up just enough to place her lips on his. So easy.

Until she heard the laughter around them, children noticing their closeness and giggling as kids were wont to do.

"Maybe another time, then?" Wade winked before dropping her hands and chasing after one of the little boys who made kissing sounds at them.

Leah laughed. She couldn't help it. Being back in skates felt good, she wasn't going to deny that. As a little girl, she dreamed of being a figure skater. It was one of the many things she'd dreamed of being until reality hit hard once her parents died.

"Confession time." Wade skated back to her side. "How many times have you put on skates since leaving Marietta?"

"Not enough," Leah confessed. She'd thought about it many times, but her schedule didn't really allow it. She lived in California because it was where the headquarters of KIND was. She shared an apartment with another employee of the charity because she was on the road more than she was home and when she did have time off, she was either back here visiting Grams and her brother or she was lying on the beach, recuperating from her latest trip.

For the next hour, Leah reveled in the feel of the ice beneath her feet, the wind in her hair, and the burn on her cheeks. She didn't stop once; not because she didn't want to, but because the lake was getting full of other skaters and she wasn't quite ready to make conversation with anyone.

That all changed when she noticed Wade sitting on the sidelines. He was having an intense conversation with someone who was gesturing wildly with their hands. Leah couldn't make out who he was talking to, but the moment she stopped in front of him and heard the voice, she knew.

Wade gave her a shake of his head. She was about to

skate away when Ethel Campton turned and pointed a finger at her.

"You."

"Mrs. Campton." Leah attempted to give her old fourth-grade teacher a smile, but faltered at the look of scorn on the woman's face.

"Don't you Mrs. Campton me, young lady. I read what you said in the paper and I'm disgusted. Disgusted." She wagged her finger at Leah with fury. "Why are you even here if you hate this town so much?"

Leah froze. Any words she'd wanted to say were stuck; they wouldn't form even if she'd wanted them to. She was hit with a sudden chill and it wrapped itself around her body, leaving her shivering.

"I wouldn't be believing everything you read in those papers, Mrs. Campton." Wade came to her defense. He held out his hand for her to take, but she couldn't.

She honestly couldn't move.

The condemnation, the judgement, and the outright anger in her old teacher's voice shocked her.

She'd expected people to be unhappy with her. She'd expected them to be upset with her.

But she hadn't been prepared for this.

"I'm sorry." If ever two words had seemed inadequate, it was those. She just didn't know what else to say.

"Harrumph." Mrs. Campton's lips thinned, and Leah could tell right away the apology wasn't enough.

"I love Marietta, I really do," Leah pleaded, needing to be believed.

"You could have fooled me. It was one thing for you to move away, but you work with that charity and kids need to spread their wings." Mrs. Campton breathed in deep and let out a long, long sigh. "But to turn your back on the town that basically raised you after your poor parents were killed...that hurts, Leah Morgan. It hurts a lot."

"I never meant for that to happen. It's not how I feel and—"

"But you said it, did you not?" Mrs. Campton interrupted her before she turned to Wade. "I don't believe everything I read, but if she said it..."

"I said it." Leah owned up to it. It didn't matter how it came out; it didn't matter that it was taken out of context and that the editing made it sound worse than it was. She'd said it, and that was all Mrs. Campton...all of Marietta...cared about.

Her admission seemed to stop Mrs. Campton short.

"Then...then why are you here? Why did you come back to a place that used to be your home?"

Leah caught the emphasis on *used to be*.

"It still is."

"You have a funny way of showing it." Mrs. Campton crossed her arms, not giving Leah an inch.

Wade's hand was still outstretched and Leah finally took it, accepting his help off the lake and to the bench where her boots waited for her.

Her toes were now frozen along with the rest of her, and she wasn't sure if her hands shook from the cold or from the shock of Mrs. Campton's words as she untied her skate laces.

"I understand why you're upset." Leah licked her cracked lips. "I'd like to attempt to explain."

"No," Wade spoke up. "You don't need to explain. People should know you better. They do know you better." The muscle in his tight jaw clenched as he stuck his fisted hands into his jacket pockets. "They should believe in what they know, not what they read."

"Wade." Leah reached out to stop him.

"Well, I'll…" Mrs. Campton held her hands up to her chest.

"What about giving her the benefit of doubt?" Wade continued as if neither she nor her old teacher had spoken. "Is it too much to ask that you put your faith in someone you know rather than those gossip magazines that only hype things up for sales?" He rubbed his fingers through his hair in frustration, and it did Leah's heart a world of good to see him stand up for her.

But she didn't need him to.

"Mrs. Campton." Leah stood. "You deserve an explanation." She pushed past the lump that was stuck in her throat. "In fact, the whole town deserves an explanation. But I don't have one. I wish I did. All I have is an apology. It's hard to fight against something everyone can read and hear on their own, and no matter what I say or how much I try to explain…" She dropped back down onto the bench. "I don't think it'll matter."

"The truth always matters," Mrs. Campton said, surprising Leah.

She looked up, searching the older woman's eyes. "The truth is, I said a lot of things I regret. The show I was on edited them to make them sound worse than they were, but, regardless, I still said the words. My heart…" She looked toward Wade before looking away again. "My heart was broken, and I lashed out."

"That's not the whole truth," Wade added.

Leah closed her eyes at his words. No, it wasn't the whole truth, but it was the only truth that mattered right now. Nothing she said or did would ever truly explain what happened or even excuse it. She needed to make peace with that.

Just like she had to make peace with the fact there was no future for her and Wade. Not together, at least.

"It's the only one that matters."

Mrs. Campton stepped toward her and reached for her hands. Her expression softened as she did so.

"I'm sorry, Leah. Your young man is right. I do know you better, and I should have had more faith in you. I don't know what I was thinking."

Leah accepted the apology although there was no need for it. "You were thinking what everyone else is thinking, and it's okay." She looked at their joined hands and appreciated the gesture.

"Leah…"

She looked toward Wade and could read on his face what he was asking. Was she okay?

Honestly? No. She just wanted to go home.

"I'm sorry, Mrs. Campton, that I've disappointed you and let you down—that I've let Marietta down." She withdrew her hands and stuffed her feet into the yellow rain boots.

Why had she thought running home to Marietta would be okay? That it would be a safe place? She should have known better. Should have realized word would spread and people would believe whatever they wanted to believe, or in this case, read.

"Wade, I…can you drive me back to my brother's, please? I should probably start packing." She smoothed her coat as she stood and gathered her skates, tying the laces together.

Wade took them from her and slung them over his shoulder, along with his own.

"So you are leaving." There was a pained look in his eye that made Leah feel as if she'd betrayed him.

"Leah, dear." Mrs. Campton stopped her. "I am sorry."

Feeling as if the fiber of her core, who she was, who she thought she could be, was unraveling, Leah forced a smile on her face and thought back to when she was mourning the loss of her parents and how Mrs. Campton had been there for her, giving her a hug when she needed one, how she would pass along books she'd bought and thought Leah might like to read…she remembered the love she'd received and knew Mrs. Campton had absolutely nothing to apologize for.

"I'm the one who is sorry. But I will make it up to you and to Marietta. I don't know how but…" Without thinking, she rushed over to the woman who had shown her more love than she'd deserved and gave her a hug. "You have always been someone I've looked up to, someone I wanted to be like, and knowing I've disappointed you…I will make it up to you. I promise." She wiped away the tears that threatened to blur her vision, not caring if anyone noticed, and then rushed back toward Wade's truck.

The drive back to Dylan's home was a quiet one. Wade barely looked at her the whole ride home.

"Thanks for bringing me skating," Leah said quietly to break the silence. "It's been too long since I've been on skates."

"If you stay, we could go skating again."

Leah noted Wade's tight grip on the steering wheel and the way he kept his focus straight ahead. "Maybe next time I come back," she offered.

He pulled up outside Dylan's house and turned the truck off.

"Do you need a ride to the airport tomorrow?" He angled toward her, his one arm resting on the back of the seats.

She heard the wistfulness in his voice, the regret of something not there, and it hurt. Her bruised heart couldn't take anymore. She couldn't pretend that things were the same between them, because they weren't.

Things hadn't been the same since she'd told him she hoped that she wasn't too late, that she was in love with him, and, after a lengthy pause, he'd said goodbye.

There was no going back from that. No matter how much she wished it.

"Dylan's giving me a ride." She reached for the handle and pushed the door open.

"Leah..." Wade's voice stopped her. "What's happened between us?" He rubbed the back of his neck and frowned. "I thought you were planning on moving back, that you were ready to come home...back to Marietta. But now when you say home, I know you're talking about California. What happened? What changed? Was it something I did or didn't do? Did I give you too much space? Is it all this nonsense with *Charmed* and—"

"Wade." Leah let all the hurt that swirled inside of her from today be heard in her voice. She hopped out of the truck and gripped the door until it dug into her palm. "Things changed; it happens and you gotta roll with it. Isn't that what you always say? Marietta isn't my home, not anymore, and you..." She looked away and blinked her eyes really hard to stop the tears. "What happened is my fault." It was hard to admit that, but it was time to accept the truth. "I took you for granted, and I thought you'd always be there. I'm not sure if I can go back to what we had."

Her voice cracked from the tears she tried so hard to push away. She turned before he could say anything, before she made even more of a fool of herself, and closed the door behind her.

She heard him calling for her, but she wouldn't turn; she couldn't. Maybe she was being a chicken, taking the easy way out, not talking this through with Wade…and if so, that was fine.

She'd told him she loved him and he made it very clear he didn't return her feelings, not anymore.

The last thing she wanted to hear was an explanation why. She didn't want to see the pity in his eyes, hear the apology in his voice, or feel what it meant to have her heart crushed all over again.

She would leave tomorrow and figure out a way to live her life without Wade in it. She had to.

Chapter Twelve

LEAH'S CHEEKS FLAMED as she sank down in a corner chair, a mug of hot tea in her hand.

"Are you going to tell me what happened today?" Dylan sat on the couch on the other side of the room. He set the book he'd been reading beside him and studied her.

Leah buried her nose in her mug, breathing in the sweet aroma and let her scraggly hair hang over her face. She was a mess. The backside of her pants was damp from falling a few times on the ice, her hair in disarray. She couldn't stop shaking, and it wasn't from the cold.

The weight of everything hit her the moment she stepped into Dylan's house and closed the door behind her. She stood there, eyes clenched shut, until the sound of Wade's truck drove away. The moment she could no longer hear the truck, the splintered pieces of her heart, the ones she'd thought she'd glued back together, fell apart.

He was gone.

"Where do you want me to start? The talking to I got from Grams? The phone call from Betsy? The whispers at the lake? Or when Mrs. Campton told me how disappointed in me she was?" She was so ready to leave, to head back to her cozy little apartment where there was no snow, no cold, and no Wade.

"How about you start with Wade driving away and you crying at my front door?" Dylan gave the appearance of being calm, relaxed, and casual, but his fingers drummed on his knee which was a dead giveaway that he was more than just a little bothered.

He never did like to see her cry. It always stressed him out, even when they were kids.

"What did he say to you?" The speed of his drumming increased.

"It wasn't so much what he said but what he didn't say. Or maybe what I didn't say." Leah rubbed her hand over her face. "Gah, I don't know...it's just not the same anymore, Dylan. I..." She could feel the tears coming back, and neither of them wanted that. "I waited too long, I expected too much, and I was too late."

"Too late for what? For Wade? That man will wait forever for you, and you know it."

She took a sip of her tea and made a wish as she inhaled.

She wished forever was still possible, even when she knew forever was in the past.

"I wish that were true, Dylan, I really do. But when I told him I loved him, he literally gave me the brush off."

"He what?" Dylan sat on the edge of the couch and

looked at her in surprise. "I find it hard to believe he would do that."

"Once upon a time, I would have thought the same thing. Karma sucks. I took Wade for granted, I thought he'd be there for me, waiting until I was ready, but I was wrong." Leah set her tea down on the coffee table and sank down in the chair until her head rested comfortably against the back of it. Her legs were pulled up and off to the side and if it weren't for the hot bath calling her name, she would close her eyes and sleep for a few minutes.

"Have you talked to him about it since being home?" Dylan asked.

She shook her head. "It's the elephant in the room between us. He probably doesn't want to embarrass me, and I don't need a reminder of what I've lost."

Dylan pushed himself up from the couch and held out his hand to her. "I think you're blind and making the situation more than it is. Talk to him, but after you have that bath. I hate seeing you shiver."

She let herself be pulled up and then into a big bear hug.

"You're both too stubborn for your own good," he muttered before releasing her.

"Not stubborn." She felt the sadness of the situation seep in. "Just...facing reality, I guess." She took his advice and headed toward the stairs. A hot bath in that large claw-foot tub was exactly what she needed.

"It's no different than with you and Casey. When was

the last time you talked with her?" Leah said over her shoulder.

Casey Michaels had been—still was—Dylan's soul mate. She knew it. He knew it. Heck, everyone in Marietta knew it…almost like they knew her and Wade were meant to be together.

Except, just like her and Wade, it was never the right time.

"That's different and you know it." The lines on his forehead deepened at the mention of Casey's name. "I talked with her a few months ago, I think."

"Guess being stubborn runs in the family, huh?" Leah marched up the stairs and didn't bother to wait around for him to reply.

Why did men think it was so easy? Why did everyone in this town seem so surprised when she admitted she was too late with Wade? And since when did men think it was a good idea to talk? While she ran the hot water, Leah fumed at the audacity of her brother to assume that she was in the wrong, that she was over exaggerating, and all it would take was a sit down and chat to clear the air?

Okay, okay, maybe he hadn't quite said that, but she knew he was thinking it.

She turned off the water, wrapped a warm robe around herself, and marched back downstairs to give her brother a piece of her mind. There was no way she was going to enjoy that bath until she did.

"Dylan, since when did you become Mr. Matchma…" She stopped mid-sentence as she walked into the kitchen and caught her brother on the phone.

"Anyway, Casey, I'll ah…" He half-turned toward Leah, his cheeks blazing bright red. "I'll try calling back at another time. Hope you're well." He set his phone down on the counter and shrugged.

"I can't give you advice if I don't follow it myself, right?" he said sheepishly.

Leah dashed across the room and wrapped her arms around her brother, giving him a big hug.

"What's this for?" he asked.

"Cause you're the best brother a girl could ask for." She rose on her tiptoes to give him a kiss on the cheek.

"You were going to yell at me, weren't you?" He could read her like a book.

She snagged a cookie from a platter on the counter and took a bite. "Maybe." She rushed back up the stairs to her waiting bath.

While she soaked, she thought about her brother. He always seemed so strong, capable, happy with his lot in life, but she'd heard something in his voice when he was on the phone—loneliness.

She never thought of Dylan as being lonely and that bothered her.

Like Wade, had she taken advantage of her brother? Assumed he was okay, happy living in Marietta, content with the way things turned out?

She remembered what he'd been like the last time Casey had come into town for a visit with her parents. Leah had stopped in between schools and found the two of them having a picnic with Grams at the park by St. James Church. Dylan had laughed with ease and wore a constant smile the entire time Leah had been there.

The relationship between Dylan and Casey was one of a kind. They were soul mates through and through. Leah had once asked Dylan why they weren't together, and he'd said it wasn't their time yet.

It was the *yet* that she always thought about. To her, yet meant that it would be their time—one day. *Yet* meant he was patiently waiting. *Yet* meant that there was hope.

It was what she'd held on to when it came to her and Wade. It hadn't been their time—*yet*. She wasn't ready—*yet*.

Maybe she'd been wrong.

Wrong to wait. Wrong to assume he'd always be there. Wrong to think there would be time.

She lightly rubbed her chest where it felt bruised from emotional scarring and sank further in the bath water, until the bubbles tickled her nose.

What was it with baths and heartbreak?

Little over a month ago, she'd called Wade from the bath…she could have waited until after, but the need and desire to talk with him, to hear his voice, to share her heart, had been too overwhelming.

They'd chatted a little bit, shared their day—she'd just returned from a hectic two-week schedule of speaking in high schools throughout Texas, and he was packing for a weeklong hiking trip into the mountains with a tour from Cincinnati.

She'd delayed as long as her nerves would allow before blurting out everything within her heart.

How sorry she was it had taken her so long, how she realized this wasn't the life she wanted—alone and only being friends—that she was in love with him and had been for a very long time, only she had been too afraid to admit it.

By the time she'd finished, there'd been only silence on the other end of the phone before Wade cleared his throat and said he should probably go, that he had an early morning and needed to finish packing his supplies, but he'd call her when he got back, okay?

She'd whispered okay, her heart literally breaking into pieces as she did so before she hung up and bawled like a baby until the tub water had grown cold.

Dylan suggested talking to him. About what? About her mistake? About him not waiting? About her being a basket case on television and now everyone knew it? Or if they didn't...they would as soon as the episode aired.

And Betsy wanted to film her some more? Lonely Leah Finds Love?

What a joke.

DYLAN WAS SITTING at the kitchen table, laptop in front of him, when she came down the stairs.

"Feeling better?" Dylan quickly shut the screen of his laptop.

"Warmer, at least." She stepped to the stove where a pot of soup simmered. "I knew I smelled chicken noodle. Did you make this?"

He shook his head. "Fundraiser at the school; I bought a bunch of frozen soups and casseroles."

She swirled the spoon in the soup before replacing the lid. "Do you eat alone a lot?" She pulled out slices of bread and placed them in the toaster. There was nothing better than buttered toast with chicken noodle soup.

"Enough." He shrugged. "Grams comes over a few times a week and plays around in the kitchen or we'll go out for dinner, but the majority of the time, it's just me."

"I'm sorry," Leah said.

"For what?" He gave her a confused glance while twisting in his chair to get a better look at her.

She relaxed her hands on the counter behind her and gave him a soft smile.

"What? What am I missing?"

She shook her head slowly. "Nothing. I just..." She struggled with the words. "Life is so busy sometimes, you know? I think I forgot that I'm not the only lonely one out there."

Lonely Leah. The media sure got that name right. She

doubted she'd be able to live it down either.

"I'm not lonely." Dylan got up from the table and went to the island, across from her. "Is that what you think of me? Here in this house, all alone?"

Honestly? Yes, that was exactly what she thought.

"You're not dating anyone. You spend evenings with Grams, you DJ at the radio station, and you have people taking bets on how badly you forecast the weather. Am I wrong to assume you're not living the life you want to be living?"

The look on his face said exactly that.

"This is the life you want to be living?"

Dylan snagged the last cookie on the plate and broke it in half.

"What's wrong with my life? I have a job that I find fun, I have friends who know how to make me laugh when I screw up, and I make sure our grandmother isn't lonely. At least I didn't run away from Marietta the moment I could without looking back." He offered her half the cookie, which she refused to take.

"I didn't mean it like that," he backtracked, forcing the cookie into her hand. "I'm happy here. I don't need more from life, and that's okay with me. Besides, don't make this about me when we both know it's really about you."

Leah pinched the bridge of her nose. "About me? How so?"

"Why don't you tell me about Betsy's phone call?" Dylan

sat back down at the table and pushed the other chair out with his foot.

Like a good sister, Leah took the hint and sat down.

"How did you know about Betsy's call?" Leah frowned. The only person who knew about it was Sage...

"You told me. Earlier. You got a talking to from Grams, which I can only imagine being about the crap in the papers today, and then you said Betsy called."

Leah ground her teeth before she hid her head in her hands. "She's going to ruin my life."

Dylan chuckled. "You're only realizing that now? At least she keeps you on your toes."

Leah looked up and was about to argue when she stopped herself. He was right. Every single thing that had ended poorly, made her look like a fool, had gotten her in sticky messes...were all centered around Betsy and her bright ideas.

"Why didn't you say anything?" Leah groaned.

He chuckled again. "I'm pretty sure both Grams and I have said stuff. You just don't listen. Anyway, what's she done now? Doesn't she realize you need a bit of a break to recoup after the mess she put you in?"

"She wants to send a crew from *Charmed* up here to do a special follow up and call it *Lonely Leah Finds Love* or something equally as ridiculous." Ten dollars it was Betsy who came up with that line too—she wouldn't put it past her.

The look on her brother's face was priceless. He stared at her with a mixture of exasperation and disbelief.

"I know." She shook her head. "Believe me, I know."

"No, it's actually brilliant." Dylan grabbed a can of soda from the fridge and opened it. "Think about it—they want the focus to be on you and Wade, since you did confess your undying love for him," he said.

"Thanks for the reminder." Leah covered half her face with the palm of her hand.

"But we turn the tables and have them focus on the town instead." His animated hands flapped in the air, something he often did when excited by a new idea. "Sure, they're going to follow you and Wade around, but they're gonna do a little bit on Marietta, to set the scene and stuff. So, we help them. We show all the good parts of Marietta, the rodeo, the scavenger hunt, the people…heck, we can even introduce them to Sage's chocolates. That's free publicity right there for her. This could be good, Leah, really good."

He sat back down at the table and started to type rapidly on his computer.

"What…what are you doing?" She didn't like this, didn't like how excited he was—like a dog with a bone or a hamster on a wheel. She knew her brother. Once he got hold of an idea, he didn't stop until it became reality.

She wasn't going to be an idea.

She wasn't going to help him make it a reality.

She wasn't going to be here in Marietta, period.

"I'm making a list. Places they can shoot, things we want highlighted. We should talk to the mayor—"

"Wait." She stood behind him and squeezed his shoulder. "I'm leaving in the morning, remember?"

His fingers stopped with their tap-tap-tapping, and he looked up at her.

"Stay."

She shook her head.

"You have to stay. You can't leave now." He twisted in his seat and covered her hand with his. "Don't you see, Leah, this is the answer. For making everything right, for righting your wrong, as unintentional as it was. This is how you apologize to the town. And let's face it, you…"

"Need to apologize," she finished for him. She knew he was right, but she'd think of another way. Not like this.

Not with *Charmed* here digging into everyone's closets, because that was exactly what would happen.

Not by pretending something that wasn't there was there…there was no happily-ever-after for her.

Not when she was supposed to be keeping her head down before heading back to work.

Not going to happen.

"You're kind of out of options here, kiddo." Dylan squeezed her hand one more time before letting go.

Kiddo. He would call her that when he was trying to parent her—at least, it was what he did growing up.

It was something her father used to call her, when he was

still alive.

"There's always more options; you just need to give them time to appear." That was something their mother used to say.

"Normally, I'd agree with you, but time doesn't seem to be on your side right now."

She ground her teeth. He was right. "You know, Karma can just bite my—"

"Whoa. Careful." Dylan laughed at her. He stood and gave her a hug, something she needed right now.

"I'm going to miss you," she mumbled against his chest.

"Then don't leave."

Don't leave. If only that were possible. Why couldn't he understand the reasons why she couldn't stay?

Seeing Wade, being close to him, spending time with him…it hurt. Hurt a lot.

If things had been different between them, she'd stay in a heartbeat.

In a *heartbeat*.

Chapter Thirteen

LEAH WAS LEAVING tomorrow.

How was that happening?

From the moment he found out she was back in town—and not by her—it'd been a train wreck.

Ever since that one night, things had gone downhill between them. No matter what he tried to do, to say, there was nothing he could do to fix things.

He needed to fix things. It was what he did. It was who he was.

So why couldn't he fix whatever was going on between them?

He'd thought going skating yesterday would help, but not only did he find out she was leaving him—well, Marietta, but it might as well be him—but there'd been the whispers, the chats, and then Ethel Campton.

Why did he have to talk to Ethel Campton?

He blamed the whole debacle on himself. He hadn't protected Leah like he should have.

Wade looked at the dollhouse he was building for the

Saturday night raffle during rodeo season in the autumn. It was a hobby of his—building things for kids and giving them away. Since dropping Leah off at the house, he'd grabbed his tool belt and focused on the little jobs he'd been putting off, like fixing the radiator in his house, changing the outside lights, adding planter hooks to the front porch for the flower pots he bought every spring…anything to keep his mind off the fact Leah was leaving.

He'd sent her a few texts, casual at first, but then outright asking if he could see her to talk—but he'd gotten no response.

Was this the brush-off he'd always feared would happen?

Years ago, he'd bared his heart and told her exactly how he'd felt. He'd hoped she felt the same way, or at least might give it some thought, but she'd put him down—gently—but it still hurt nonetheless. He'd promised her he would never tell her how he felt again, would never say the words he longed to whisper in her ear, until she was ready.

He'd always hoped one day she would be.

He wanted to tell her he loved her with every molecule of his soul. He needed to tell her, but he promised he wouldn't.

So, he showed her. At least, he thought he had.

He'd thought she'd noticed. It seemed like it a few months ago. She teased him about their pending trip, they talked more often than usual, and she'd even hinted that she was ready for a change, that she could see herself moving back home. That she wanted to talk to her boss at KIND about using Marietta as her home base.

She'd said it was all her fault…but what? What was her fault?

He couldn't wrap his head around that.

He dropped the sander in his hand and made a decision. If she wasn't going to respond to his text messages, then he was going to go see her in person. If she was that determined to not talk to him, she could tell him so herself.

He was tired of all these games. Tired of not knowing what was going on. Tired of trying to read her mind— something he obviously sucked at.

Dylan was outside throwing sand on the sidewalk and walkway from the house when he pulled up.

"Hey," Dylan greeted him as he rounded the truck. "About time you showed up."

"Your sister seems to be ignoring me." Maybe Dylan could shed some light on things, or at least give him a heads-up if he was about to enter a war zone.

"She's always had a hard time saying goodbye."

"Then maybe she should stop leaving." Wade scuffed his boots on the walkway to check out the layer of sand.

"I do know how to shovel," Dylan said, catching him in the act.

"What happened to all the snow and ice melting by this afternoon?" He couldn't let an opportunity to tease Dylan pass him by.

"Yeah, yeah." Dylan waved him off. "If you're thinking

of talking her out of leaving, I might have some info for you first. But keep it up, wise guy, and my lips are sealed." Dylan finished sanding and set the pail down by the front stair.

"Loved the snow that fell. Couldn't skate if everything melted." Wade was quick with his reply. Any info on Leah was good info.

"Betsy wants to bring a crew up and do a feature on Leah here in Marietta."

By the pinch between Dylan's brows, Wade wasn't sure if the feature was a good or bad idea. "But she's leaving tomorrow." Right? Or had that changed?

"Maybe you'll have better luck talking her out of it than I did."

This time, it was Wade who frowned. "What am I missing?"

Dylan rubbed his chin. "They want to call it *Lonely Leah Finds Love*."

Wade scowled. He hated the nickname they gave her on the show. Hated what it said about her, how it described her, and what it obviously made her feel.

She was anything but alone. Why didn't she see that?

"Yeah, that was her reaction. What is up with you two? I thought you loved her, man. Why did you push her away? She's not staying because of you—did you know that?"

Sucker punched in the gut, Wade could barely catch his breath.

Push her away? Leaving because of him?

"I don't understand." He reached for the rail on the steps and gripped hard. "What are you talking about?"

"My sister went crazy on television and confessed you broke her heart...and you have no idea what I'm talking about?" Dylan crossed his arms and pierced Wade with one of those *you-hurt-my-sister-now-die* looks.

"Broke her heart? Dude, I really have no idea what you're talking about. Is that why she's been so cagey and offish with me? Why she won't talk to me?" He wracked his brain trying to think of a time when he'd done that—broke her heart—but nothing came to mind.

He would remember if she told him she loved him.

"It was before you did that one trip into the mountains with the folks from Cincinnati. Remember? The ones I picked up from the airport because you were running late."

It was also the last time he'd spoken on the phone with Leah. But she'd said nothing...

"Ahh, you do remember." Dylan punched him in the arm, hard.

"What was that for?" Wade rubbed his arm. For a desk jock, the guy could throw a good punch.

"My sister told you she loved you, and you hung up the bloody phone. What do you think it was for?"

No way. "I'm pretty sure I would know if Leah said the words I've been waiting years to hear." He looked up at the house, hoping for a glance of her. What was Dylan talking about? She'd never said...

Toward the end of the call, there'd been a lot he hadn't heard.

His gut twisted and his heart swelled like a rooster about to crow with the possibilities of all the things he *hadn't* heard her say.

"You heard me about the Betsy and her crew part, right?" Dylan nudged him with his foot.

Wade tore his gaze from the Leah's bedroom window. "What about Betsy?"

Dylan chuckled. "Say the word love and you're a lost cause, aren't you? Betsy wants to come and do a feature on Leah and you—on the love you both share. Except Leah won't do it because you turned her down."

"But I—"

Dylan stopped him. "You didn't turn her down. Yeah, yeah, I get it. Except she thinks you did and so she refuses to stay. But having that film crew could be good for Marietta. It could also work wonders for Leah getting back in everyone's good graces once they find out what she said."

Wade let that sink in. Good for Marietta and for Leah, but only if she stayed in town.

"And you want me to...what?"

The man in question snorted like a pig waiting for its slop. "Do I really need to spell it out?"

Wade looked back at the house. Her window had grown dark, but the light to the stairs was now on.

No, he didn't need it spelled out.

"Why don't you tell that sister of yours to come out here and tend to her snowmen? Someone's been eating their noses." A smile grew across Wade's face. He dislodged the carrots from the snow, put one in his pocket, and took a bite out of the other.

"Good chatting with you, man." Dylan bounded up the stairs and opened the door, calling to Leah before closing it.

Wade mulled over everything while he chewed on that carrot. He was leaning against his truck when Leah came outside, the scarf he'd knitted her wrapped around her neck.

"Wade? Why are you here?" She slowly climbed down the stairs and made her way toward him. "Is that a...carrot?" she asked when he took another bite.

He reached into his pocket and took out the other one, handing it to her. "Hungry?" He just wanted to see a smile on her face and ease the tension in her shoulders. She radiated stress, and he wanted that to change. Starting now.

"You never did join me for our late-night owl watching session." He thought that might bring a smile to her face, the memories of all those nights outdoors, binoculars in hand... Their best conversations were in the woods when it was just the two of them, the darkness, and only the animals to keep them company.

But that smile never showed up.

"Maybe next time," she said softly. There was a sadness there he wanted to erase.

Strike that. He *was* going to erase it.

"We both know that if you leave tomorrow morning, the chances of there being another time are slim."

He caught the flash of honesty in her eyes before she looked away and stared off into the dark.

She wasn't going to deny it, and he appreciated that.

"Are you here to say goodbye?" Her voice carried in the cool wind that blew. It was another sucker punch. He wasn't sure how much more he could take tonight.

"No. I'm here to talk you out of leaving. Your brother—"

"No."

"Let me finish." He didn't move, didn't raise his voice, didn't do anything but smile.

"I'm not staying," she repeated.

"Will you let me finish?"

He waited, watched her look everywhere but at him until she finally stood beside him, leaned against the truck, and held out her hand.

He handed her the carrot with a smile and took that as a yes, he could finish.

"I think taking Betsy up on her suggestion is a smart move. Not just for you, but for Marietta. You could really do this town a favor by letting that camera crew come in and do whatever it is they do. So many businesses here could use the boost, and they've got to stay somewhere, right? From what I hear, the Bramble House is empty right now and, well, you know Josie would shine in the spotlight. Do you really want to take that from her?"

"Bringing Grams into this is not playing fair."

Wade's smile grew even wider, to the point where it started to hurt. "Darlin', I think the time for playing fair is over, don't you?"

The look on her face was priceless. He wiped the smug smile off his face and tried to act serious when all he wanted to do was jump for joy.

He'd honestly thought her saying she was already in love with someone on television was a ploy, that it was a way for her to get off the show. In fact, he'd even texted her that after finding out she went on it without realizing she didn't have her phone. But if Dylan was being honest...he was the one she was in love with and that changed everything for him.

"Wade, as much as I agree with you, my brother, and even Sage about how good this could be for Marietta, I *can't* stay. You, of all people, should understand that."

She sounded distressed.

If Wade was a gentleman, he would take away all his angst and save her the embarrassment...but he couldn't.

He'd made a promise to her that he wouldn't share how he felt again until she did so first. And, despite being told she already had, he needed to hear it from her directly.

So, the goal was to get her to admit it.

"Refresh my mind, Leah. Why exactly can't you stay?"

She grunted with obvious frustration and stamped her boot on the ground. "Don't do this," she said between clenched teeth.

It took all his strength not to smile.

She looked so cute standing there, arms crossed over her chest as she stared at the ground.

He gently placed his fingers beneath her chin and forced her to look at him. "You've been talking in circles since you've gotten here. How about you just tell me straight?"

"I have *not* been talking in circles. You know exactly what I'm talking about, so you can wipe that smile off your face." Leah's lips pursed into a tiny white line. Uh-oh. The last thing he wanted to do was get her mad at him. "I don't get why you think this is so funny," she muttered.

"What I find amusing is the way you've been avoiding me."

"I'm not avoiding you!" Her fist pounded against the side of his truck.

"Easy there," Wade said. "Abigail doesn't like being mistreated." He winked, hoping to ease the tension that was between them. It must have worked because he caught the way Leah glanced at him out of the corner of her eye.

"It's either her or you." Leah looked straight ahead, but Wade caught the slight movement of her lips.

She was trying not to smile.

"There's many things I love about you, Leah girl, but you hitting Abigail isn't one of them. Next time, hit me. I'm a big boy, I can handle it."

She startled at his use of love. Good. He was going to say

it more often too rather than work hard not to say it.

It amazed him how easily it slid off his tongue. Like honey. Or, rather, like biting into a piece of Sage's chocolate and having it melt into a gooey mess of goodness.

Love. He loved her. There was something about her that made him feel alive—just her presence, the way she talked and was animated by life in general. The way she moved reminded him of a ballerina—both on and off the ice. He'd taken Josie and a few of her friends to the city last year to watch the Nutcracker Ballet, and he'd been mesmerized by the grace of the dancers. Leah reminded him of them, the way she moved, how her head always tilted while she listened to someone talk, the rigid lines of her body, yet the gracefulness of her walk. She was such a tiny thing.

"Yeah, well, there are many things I lo…like about you, too, but annoying me isn't one of them." She pushed herself away from the truck, stuck her hands in her jacket, and kicked her feet in the snow.

He'd heard like, but he knew it was forced.

She'd wanted to say love; he knew she did.

"I'll take annoyance over the way you've been with me lately." Wade looked her solidly in the eye, not breaking contact with her, daring her to look away. "If I hadn't been here waiting for you earlier today, you probably wouldn't have come skating, would you have? You would have found some excuse to not see me at all and that hurts, Leah. It hurts deep."

"And that went so well, didn't it." She continued to hold his gaze. He could see a bit of fire in her eyes, and it was exactly what he wanted to see.

Her leaving tomorrow equaled her running away, and running was something Leah never did. Ever.

She was one of the strongest women he knew.

"I think it went fine. Sure, you got some backlash over what's being said about you, but you knew that was going to happen. Ethel stopped by Kindred House afterward to talk to Josie, did you know that?"

Leah's shoulders slumped. "What did she say?"

"That she was sorry she'd been so hard on you earlier. She'd hoped you were there, to be honest. I think Josie thought you might as well. She's missed you."

"Maybe I'll bring Grams out to stay with me for a while after I'm home." Leah let out a very long and weary sigh. Perhaps the thought of leaving hurt her as much as it did him.

"Or you could just stay and make this your home." He paused for a moment. "Like we'd talked about before."

She swallowed hard. "That was before. You know that."

"Before what?" He wanted her to say it, to say that she loved him. He needed to hear her say it.

"Before I realized things couldn't be the same between us. Okay?" She lifted her hands up in the air before dropping them to her side, hard. "Is that what you wanted me to say? To admit? That things can never go back to normal between us? This," she motioned between them, "this isn't working. Not anymore."

She went to walk away—to leave him again before he could say the one thing he knew she wanted to hear but was afraid he wouldn't say.

He reached for her arm and pulled her close to him. Not close enough that he could wrap his arms around her, but close enough that she could read the love in his eyes.

He hoped.

"Then let's change it. Let's make it work. Don't run from that...from me," he practically begged her.

He wasn't sure his heart could handle her leaving him. Not now. If she'd been strong enough to take a chance on him once before, hopefully she would again.

She looked at him, searched his eyes for the message he hoped she received, and then slowly placed her hand on top of his.

His chest swelled so hard he couldn't breathe. It didn't matter if she didn't say it first. Not anymore. She'd rejected him once, and he'd survived. But he knew—he knew this time she wouldn't.

"Leah, I—"

"No." The word left her mouth and hung between them, its poison weaving a web between them, separating them and tearing his heart at the same time. "We've changed, Wade, and that's okay. I've made my peace. I'm..." Her eyes clenched tight, and it looked like she fought with whatever she was about to say to him. "I'm sorry I used you like I did on the show. I took your advice and said I was in love with someone already, never realizing the damage it would do. Things have changed between us, and it's because of me. It's my fault. If I could take everything back," her voice hitched, "I would. Trust me."

Wade couldn't move. It was a miracle he even breathed. His heart dropped and shattered upon impact, the poison of her words completely destroying him.

She'd said no.

"That's not...that's not what I meant when I sent that text." Of all the things he could have said, should have said...this was all that came out.

"I'm sorry." She stood on her tiptoes and very gently laid her lips upon his stubbled cheek.

All he could think was that he should have shaved so he could feel her touch better.

He stood there, unable to move, to blink, barely able to breathe, as she turned from him and walked away.

He'd survived the last time she'd turned him down. Saying *I love you* and not having it said in return had been the worst thing that could ever happen to him.

Or so he thought.

But there'd been hope then. She at least remained in his life.

He had a feeling after tonight, she wouldn't be any longer.

Chapter Fourteen

THE LOOK IN her brother's eyes said it all.

"You think I'm making a mistake." Leah didn't bother to frame it as a question; the disappointment on his face said it all.

"Why are women so stubborn? I will never understand." There was a tortured look on his face. "You say you want love, but when there's a man in front of you with his heart in his hands, you walk away."

Was he talking about her and Wade or him and Casey?

He must have read the confusion on her face because he grunted with annoyance before walking away.

"Figures," he muttered loud enough to be heard.

"What do you mean by that?" She followed after him, not willing to let it go. If he was forcing his own issues onto her, that wasn't fair. She knew he loved Casey and that it bothered him they weren't together, but what happened between them wasn't the same as what happened...

Except it was, just in reverse.

Dylan had told Casey he loved her. She said she wasn't

ready, that she wanted a bigger life than just the small-town one he could provide.

Leah finally admitted her love to Wade and he turned her down, probably because she'd waited too long and he'd moved on.

"He doesn't love me anymore," she said, talking to his back.

"Did he say that?" Dylan confronted her, pain and anger in his gaze. "Did he come right out and say he wasn't in love with you anymore—or are you projecting something you think you heard?"

"Of course he...well, he said..." She searched her memory. Honestly, she couldn't recall him saying that specifically. He'd just ignored what she had to say and hung up.

"He didn't, did he?" Dylan challenged her.

Leah sat down on the nearest chair and rested her elbows on her knees.

The weight of realization settled on her, like a warm blanket fresh from the dryer. She could feel it all over, inside and out, and that warmth spread like wildfire, blazing straight toward her heart.

He hadn't said he didn't love her.

He hadn't said she'd waited too long.

He hadn't said that or anything else and yet...it was what she'd assumed.

Assumed he didn't love her. Assumed it was too late. Assumed so many things that possibly weren't even true.

For the first time since that dreaded phone call, she felt what it was like to hope. She'd felt the same moments before she had called him...excitement at what could happen, desire for what life could be like, and confidence that she was doing the right thing.

"Why don't you give him a chance?" Dylan set his hand on her shoulder and gave it a soft squeeze.

She looked up and knew she was going to cry. "Do you think it's too late?" There was still a sliver of fear that wanted to hold her back. What if Dylan was wrong?

Her brother chuckled before placing a kiss on the top of her head.

"Silly girl. Why don't you go unpack while I clean the kitchen, and then we can watch a movie together? Preferably nothing to do with love and everything to do with comic book heroes." He held out his hand, pulling her up and giving her one of his awesome brotherly bear hugs.

"Put the guy out of his misery while you're at it, please. At the very least, tell him you're staying."

While Dylan cleaned up the kitchen, Leah went upstairs, but not to unpack—considering she hadn't started in the first place. Instead, she went to call Betsy. When she turned on her phone, there was a message from Wade instead.

Don't leave. What we had—what we have—is more than whatever is happening right now. I've never known you to run from something before—so why are you now?

Why was she? Because she thought he didn't love her and she couldn't handle how much it hurt to be with him but not *with* him.

But she wasn't running. Not anymore.

I'm not.

She wanted to text more, but her phone rang. Betsy's name came up on her screen.

"Before you say anything, I really think you should say yes to my idea," Betsy said the moment she answered the call. "I think that it's exactly what you need. It could really good for your town. You know your grandmother loves me, and I could bring some of her favorite chocolates and—"

"Okay," Leah interrupted her.

"And I'd even bring some of the free gifts we have stashed in that closet, and hand them out to the ladies at Kindred Place and..." Betsy took a breath. "Okay? You said okay? Are you serious?"

Leah laughed. "Yes, I'm serious. Come up and bring a crew, but I have a few conditions first."

If she was going to do this, it had to be on her terms.

"Oh my God, yes! Name it and it's yours."

Leah didn't need to think too long on this. "You only get one day to film and it's to be during the St. Paddy's Day scavenger hunt. The focus will be on the town, not on me, and—"

"Whoa, girl," Betsy interrupted her. "It has to be on you.

You and Wade. That's why we're coming—*Lonely Leah Finds Love* and all that. We can do it around your town to highlight the things you want noticed, but the focus has to be on you guys as a couple."

Leah's heart rate sped up like a ticking time bomb. She needed to talk to Wade about this first. Sure, he'd said earlier he thought Betsy coming was a good idea, but he probably didn't understand what it really meant.

"Betsy..." Leah swallowed hard. "I haven't found love...yet."

"What?" Betsy yelled before she muffled her voice. "Sorry, but what? Are you kidding me? Come on, girl. What are you waiting for? I thought you said if you had the chance, you would try to mend things?"

Leah blushed, uncomfortable with the memory. She'd bawled like a baby in Betsy's arms after the taping of her falling apart and said she wanted a do-over. Except, ever since coming home, all she'd done was push Wade away.

"Leah..." Betsy drew out her name, making it very clear she was disappointed in her. "What is going on?"

Tears pricked Leah's eyes. "I pushed him away because I was afraid. But, apparently, I was wrong and he's just been waiting for me to realize it." She laughed at herself for her foolishness.

Josie, Sage, Jen Patterson, and even her brother all knew it.

She'd been the only one who couldn't see what was right

in front of her.

"So you've told him you love him?" Betsy asked.

Leah didn't answer. She wasn't sure she could say it again.

"I take it he hasn't said it either, right?"

Leah could hear the wheels turning in Betsy's mind with that one question.

"So what if we use this as your journey to finding love?"

"Journey?" Leah wasn't too sure she liked where this conversation was going.

"Exactly. Best friends afraid to admit what everyone else knows, a man who promised not to express his love until you do so, and then there's you, the girl who is afraid of being turned down again. Trust me, I can make this work and end in a happily-ever-after. It's what I do."

It's what I do. Those were the four words Leah really didn't like to hear from Betsy. She'd seen what Betsy could do, what *Charmed* was capable of.

"No. I just want it to be simple. Please? Enough damage has been done that I don't want to play any more games. I'm serious, Betsy."

First thing she needed to do was talk to Wade. And then spend a nice day together with Betsy in tow and let her create a feature that wouldn't destroy her life any more than *Charmed* already had.

"I'll undo all the damage I did. I promise."

"What did I say about your promises? One day, Betsy,"

she felt the need to remind her. Would probably need to do this over and over again, too. "We'll sample chocolates at the Copper Mountain Chocolate Shop, go ice skating, take a walk through downtown Marietta, and then enjoy the scavenger hunt. That's it. You'll get more than enough footage from that." Leah needed to remain strong, steadfast, and serious; that was the only way to stop from being railroaded like usual.

The exaggerated huff on the other end of the phone told her Betsy heard her.

"Fine. Okay, I'm going to take off the producer-of-*Charmed* hat and just talk to my best friend. Ready?"

Was Leah ready? No. She knew exactly what Betsy was going to say. She'd said it already, but Betsy wasn't one to give up until she got what she wanted.

"Lay it on me."

"You need to tell that man of yours how you feel. I'm serious."

"I know." That was exactly what she was going to do, and she couldn't wait to talk to him.

"You know? Yes!" Betsy squealed, forcing Leah to pull the phone away from her ear. "You deserve to be happy, girl. It's about time. I can't wait to hug you in person."

"When will you and the crew be here?" She needed to cancel her flight. "And just a few people, right? Not a large posse…just one or two, right?" The last thing she wanted was the full crew from *Charmed* here. Whenever they left the mansion, it was a nightmare—caravans of vehicles, hours of set up, multiple shots and frames and interviews…a simple stroll through a park to feed geese or walk through a downtown to window shop took hours to set up. There was no way she was putting the people of Marietta through that.

"This is very informal. The goal is to make it look authentic and natural, so there's only three of us. And…"

The moment Betsy paused, Leah knew to brace herself. Her stomach muscles tightened with anxiety, and she had to consciously not tighten her grip on the phone as she waited for Betsy to say something drastic, something she was known to do and often.

"What? Just say it." Leah wiggled her toes with nervous energy. How bad could it be?

"I already bought the tickets, and we'll be there noon tomorrow. I've rented a van for our equipment, but my first stop is for hot chocolate and I expect you to be there waiting for me."

Leah didn't know whether to laugh or cry or be upset that her friend would assume she was going to agree.

"What if I had left, Betsy? I would have been on my plane before you even arrived—did you think about that?" She shouldn't be surprised, though. She actually should have realized Betsy would have done this.

"Oh, you were never getting on that plane, girl. Trust me." Betsy giggled. "Josie and I had it all planned out. Dylan was going to get called away to a last-minute conference, and

Josie was going to fake a fall and beg you to stay to take care of her. I was actually kind of shocked when she mentioned the idea, to be honest. Who knew Josie had it in her?" Betsy dropped the bomb like it was nothing, like it was something they both should be laughing at.

Except she wasn't laughing. She was flabbergasted.

"You're serious? Josie was in on this? When did you talk to her? How long have you both been scheming behind my back? And my brother? What—did everyone but me know you were coming?" How could she have been so blind?

"It's not like I can just show up with a camera crew and start taping, Leah—come on. You know stuff like this takes time and preparation." Betsy couldn't stop giggling, like this was all one big joke and it was all on Leah.

She should be upset. She really should be.

"So tomorrow at Sage's, huh?" Guess she'd be bringing that gift of home-baked cinnamon buns after all.

"Tomorrow, girlfriend. See you then." Betsy hung up without so much as a goodbye. Seconds later, Leah's phone dinged with a text message.

Don't be mad. I promised you I would make it up to you, so really, you should have been expecting this. Mwah.

Leah shook her head. Yes, she should have known better.

Her phone dinged again.

PS. Changed my mind. Let your man say those magical four words first. Bet you an all-expense paid trip to Napa that he does…on Charmed's dime, of course.

PPS. I'm serious.

Chapter Fifteen

LEAH MARCHED INTO Kindred Place with a smile on her face and her hands full of a very large, very overfull tray of cinnamon buns.

Kathy noticed her first.

While wiping her hands on her apron, Kathy tsked at Leah after peeking beneath the cloth covering the gooey desserts.

"You need to stop bringing those in. I'm getting requests that they be a regular on the breakfast menu, and you know that's just not happening." However, she snagged a bun with glee and took a bite, moaning as she did so.

"Whoever taught you to make these is my hero. No chance I can get your recipe?"

Leah chuckled. "And give away my guaranteed get-out-of-jail-free card? Not in this lifetime." She peeked into the dining area and zeroed in on the one person she'd come to see.

"Ah. I've got a few of those blackmail recipes myself. Trust me when I say I've needed them a few times since working here, and your grandmother over there is the worst out of all of them." Kathy looked toward Grams sitting at one of the tables and shook her head with mock dismay.

Leah believed it. Her grandmother was known for her shenanigans.

"If I knew what was good for me, I would go offer these to everyone before they stampede over here," Leah said, except she didn't move. She was enjoying watching Grams interact with her friends. It was like she was holding court. She was the only one talking, her mouth and hands moving while everyone paid close attention.

What was she saying to them?

What stories was she telling?

Were they all in on the plan to keep her in town? Was that what Grams was sharing with them all?

One person at the table noticed her standing there, they nudged the person at their side, who then looked up. Soon, they were all looking at her rather than Josie.

"Now might be a good time." Kathy nudged her.

With a big, bright, and extra bold smile pasted on her face, Leah headed toward the table, tray in hand. She ignored all the amused glances from those around Grams, Instead, she slid the tray to the middle of the table, whisked off the cloth, and then bent down to give her dear, sweet grandmother a kiss on the cheek.

"Leah." A surprised Grams jumped in her seat, her cheeks a sudden bright red.

"My ears were ringing," Leah teased her.

"Well…ah…they should have. I was just telling everyone how you were leaving this morning." The more Grams spoke, the redder her face grew.

"Like a good granddaughter, I brought you some fresh cinnamon buns. I figured everything I'd brought yesterday would be gone."

She quite enjoyed watching Grams squirm.

"I also thought we could head for a walk before I leave. I'd hate for you to go alone and slip on any ice…the last thing you need is a broken leg or something." She couldn't quite quell the smile that appeared at the look of shock and embarrassment Grams couldn't quite hide.

"Who squealed?" Grams stood from the table, a sad look at the tray of buns Leah had brought, and entwined her arm with Leah's. "It wasn't your brother, was it?" she asked as they walked out of the dining area and down the hallway.

"Dylan never shares secrets, you know that." Leah was a little annoyed Grams would immediately assume Dylan. She should know her grandson better than that.

"I know, you're right." Grams frowned. "Betsy. It was all her idea, you know."

"Don't you do that," Leah scolded her. "Don't put the blame on anyone but yourself." Leah opened the door to Grams' apartment. "I can't believe you were going to trick me like that."

Back in her own home, Grams relaxed a little and didn't

try to appear contrite. "Well, can you really blame me, Leah Eleanor Morgan? I've been forced to trickery just to get you to stay after asking you for years to move back home. What else am I supposed to do? I'm not getting any younger, you know."

"You could just—"

"Just ask?" Grams interrupted her. "I do ask. Numerous times. I've asked in so many ways that I think you just ignore me now."

Leah wanted to argue, but Grams was right. She always did ask. And Leah always had one reason or another to say no.

"I'm sorry, Grams."

"Well." Grams huffed. "You should be. I miss you." Grams opened her arms, and Leah happily went into them.

"Don't think this excuses you though," Leah warned as she hugged her back.

"Well, if you'd listen to reason, I wouldn't have to go behind your back, now would I?"

Leah pulled away. She didn't say anything, just gave her a look, one that said seriously-how-old-are-you-again?

"Fine." Grams rolled her eyes. "I would like you to stay though, you know that, right? Seeing you three times a year is not enough. Not at my age. I could croak anytime, and—"

"Oh, don't you dare," Leah stopped her before she could say anything else. "You aren't even close to being old enough to die, and you know it." She didn't like the thought of

Grams leaving her. Not now, not ever.

"Leah, darling, if there's one thing life has taught me it's this—karma doesn't play fair, no matter how much you try to bribe, tempt, or cross your fingers and wish she did." Grams patted her arm gently and Leah leaned in to give her grandmother a kiss, knowing she was not only thinking about the child she'd lost but her husband as well.

"Grams, I fully expect you to live a very long and happy life. I will move heaven and earth to see that happen. Even if it means I need to stick around longer." Leah sat down on the couch and attempted to give the appearance of being completely relaxed.

Grams stopped in her tracks, her hand half raised. "Do you mean that?"

Leah enjoyed the look of surprise on her grandmother's face.

"Leah, if you're playing a game with me, girl..."

"I cancelled my flight this morning."

Grams launched herself and pulled Leah up into a fierce hug.

Well, if she'd known staying would elicit this kind of response...

"How long?" Grams asked, wiping her eyes as she pulled away. "And don't you dare make fun of me crying. I've missed you more than you realize."

"How long depends on a few things." She sat back down, dragging Grams along with her. If there was one thing her grandmother loved, it was scheming.

"Please tell me this has everything to do with you and Wade," Grams said.

Leah just smiled. It had everything to do with her and Wade. Betsy said Wade needed to respond to her declaration of love and, for once, Leah was in complete agreement with no hesitation. But after talking with Dylan this morning, Leah realized something she hadn't considered.

It was possible Wade hadn't heard her. And if that was true, well…that changed everything.

Everything.

"Perfect! What can I do to help?" Grams rubbed her hands together with anticipation and from the sparkle in her eye, Leah knew she already had a few ideas up her sleeve.

Chapter Sixteen

I'M NOT.

That was the last thing he'd heard from Leah.

He'd accused her of running. Running from him, from the situation she was in...from everything, and all she had to say was '*I'm not.*'

How could she not see it?

She could try to run from him. *Try* being the optimum word.

There was no way he was letting her leave Marietta without facing him.

He'd thought long and hard all night about what he would say.

He would tell her he loved her. He'd bare his heart and hope that it was enough.

He pounded on Dylan's front door and listened for the sound of her footsteps toward the door.

"Hey man, what's up?" Dylan answered, his hair a mess, face unshaven, and wearing the tackiest pair of lounge pants Wade had ever seen.

"Wonder woman?" Wade snickered. "Let me guess...gag gift?"

Hot pink with images of the Amazonian woman all over the place, the pants were no doubt meant for a woman, so it had to be a gag gift.

"My secret Santa at KCMC got revenge for a prank I pulled on her at the radio station." Dylan glanced down and shrugged. "But they're quite comfy." He stepped aside to give Wade room to enter. "If you're here for my sister, you're too late."

Wade's heart skipped a couple of beats.

"She's visiting Grams." Dylan slapped him on the shoulder, obviously noting Wade's moment of panic. "She'll be back shortly. Stick around for coffee; I just put on a fresh pot."

Wade followed Dylan into the kitchen where a plate of cinnamon buns slathered in cream cheese sat, along with a mug of coffee.

"Your sister sure has been baking a lot lately." Wade took the offered cup from Dylan and took a sip.

"She stress bakes but trust me, I'm not complaining."

Wade caught the pointed look his friend threw him. "You can't blame me for all her stress."

"Actually," Dylan said, "I can. Her reacting to what you did or didn't do is what landed her in this whole mess. So what are you going to do about it?"

Wade frowned. "I'm trying to get her to stay, that's what

I'm trying to do."

"You're doing a crappy job of it." Dylan glanced at his watch and downed his coffee. "I need to grab a shower and get ready for work, but feel free to drink more coffee and eat that cinnamon bun while you wait. She should be back soon."

Wade paused, his cup midair as Dylan's words registered.

"Wait," he called out. Dylan pivoted on his heel halfway down the hall. "I thought you were taking Leah to the airport before heading into work?"

"Yeah, and? It's not like I'm going to come home after dropping her off, you know?"

Wade felt like a fool. Of course. That made complete sense. He felt bad for questioning him in the first place. "Sorry, man. I just was kind of hoping she wouldn't be leaving, you know?"

Dylan shrugged. "I'm not the one you need to be telling, but that's why you're here, right?"

Wade nodded. That was exactly why he was here. To convince Leah to stay and give them another chance.

Twenty minutes later, Wade was still sitting there when Dylan came back down from his shower.

"She not home yet?" Dylan sounded surprised.

"No." Wade knew he sounded like a petulant teenager, but he didn't care. Normally, he was a patient man, but today was not a normal day.

"Why haven't you gone to find her then? It's not like you

don't know where she is," Dylan said.

Wade scowled. He'd thought about that but every time he'd gotten up to leave, he stopped himself. He knew how much Josie missed Leah, and he didn't want to intrude on what little time they had left together.

"Go and get her, will you? Tell her to get her butt back here cause we need to leave."

Wade shrugged on his jacket and headed toward the front door. He turned and was about to open his mouth, but Dylan stood there and shook his head.

"Women, they don't make sense. I feel for you, I really do. I know what it's like to watch the one person you love more than life walk away from you. I wish I had the answer for you, but I don't. So, I'm here if you need to talk. I've also got a basement to tear apart if you ever need to join me."

"Thanks. I'll probably end up taking you up on that." There was a sick feeling in his gut every time he thought about Leah leaving, and it only intensified the longer he waited to talk to her. He didn't know how Dylan did it. Wade remembered how raw Dylan had been when Casey left. He'd gone into the woods and camped out for a solid week before returning to town.

He headed toward Kindred Place and literally ran to Josie's apartment only to find it empty. He searched the house for her, but she wasn't in the dining area or the craft room or the library where she liked to sit and read in front of the fireplace. He asked people as he passed them in the hallway but other than seeing Leah earlier in the morning with a plate of cinnamon buns, they had no idea where she'd gone.

He wasn't going to panic. He called Leah's cell phone, fully not expecting her to pick up. When she did, he hesitated.

"Wade? This isn't another one of your butt dials, is it?"

The sound of Leah's laughter, the lighthearted, carefree sound, eased the panic in his heart.

"Hey." One word, one pathetic word, but it was all he could muster.

"Oh hey, you're actually there. I was about to hang up. What's up?"

What's up? Was this the same girl who'd pushed him away all week? The same girl who was running away from him, from what they shared? The same girl who said what they had was no longer there?

"Wade?"

"Where are you?" He heard a murmur of voices in the background, and several locations went through his mind. She'd taken Josie to the grocery store. They were having breakfast at the diner, or possible enjoying a cup of cocoa at Sage's shop.

As long as she wasn't at the airport, that was all he really cared about.

"I'm sipping the best cocoa in the county...oops, sorry, in our country, while helping Sage finish up her coins. Come join us," Leah suggested.

*Come join us...*he couldn't ask for a better invite.

"See you soon." He couldn't stop grinning after he hung up and jogged to his truck.

She sounded different. It wasn't that she was with Sage and putting on a front; she actually sounded...like his Leah. Like his Leah who called him while in the bathtub and just wanted to hear his voice. Like his Leah who suggested an alternate to their trip to Napa. Like his Leah who had talked of a future for the two of them in Marietta.

Maybe...maybe it wasn't too late for them after all. Maybe she realized what they had, maybe she was ready to say those words he so wanted to hear, needed to hear.

But, as much as he wanted to hope, to believe...he tampered all those emotions that bubbled deep within him.

This wasn't the Leah he'd watched walk away from him yesterday after the whole skating incident. Something was up.

He found a place to park down the street from the chocolate shop. When he opened the door, he was surprised at the crowd in the room. The tables were full, and there was even a line at the counter.

"Hey Wade, it's about time you showed up." Sage gave him a wave from where she stood at the cash register.

Portia looked up and gave him a smile before she continued to fill a box of chocolates for a customer.

The only ones Wade recognized in the store were Sage, Portia, Leah, and Betsy. Everyone else wasn't from Marietta.

Maybe…wait, Betsy?

What was she doing here?

Leah's face was bright red as he headed toward her. She looked from Betsy to him and then down at her cup before he caught her taking a deep breath and forcing a smile on her face.

Ahh…that was what was up.

It wasn't his Leah who had spoken on the phone.

She's been putting on a front for Betsy.

Wade squashed the disappointment and heartache at the realization.

For a moment, he'd let hope resurface but he should have known better.

"Betsy, good to see you," Wade said as he pulled out the chair and sat. There was a full cup of cocoa in front of him. "I'm hoping this is mine and not meant for someone else." He pasted a smile on his face, determined not to let his disappointment show.

"I asked Sage to make you one as soon as I hung up." Leah's voice was soft, breathy, but Wade put up a wall to protect his heart.

"I'd forgotten how much I love Sage's cocoa." Betsy giggled before she took a long sip of hers. The tip of her nose was covered in whipped cream. Leah passed her a napkin while rolling her eyes.

"I thought," Wade ignored Betsy for the moment, "you were leaving this morning?" He watched the slight flutter to

Leah's lashes, how she looked away and fought the rise of her lips. "Dylan's waiting for you," he added as a reminder.

He enjoyed watching the flush on her face rise.

When Leah pulled out her phone and her fingers flew over the keyboard, he assumed she was texting her brother. He waited patiently for her to finish, his gaze never leaving her face. He knew Betsy was laughing at him, and as much as it bothered him to be the subject of whatever inside joke was going on…he pretended like it didn't matter.

As long as Leah was staying, he didn't care about the reason.

He could guess it, however—especially with Betsy sitting right beside him.

Either Leah had agreed to do the feature or Betsy came believing she could convince her better face to face. He tended to believe the latter.

Once Leah had put her phone away, they sat there in silence. It took everything inside Wade not to speak up, to ask her outright what was going on.

Thankfully, he didn't have to wait long.

"Guess you're wondering why Betsy's here?" Leah finally spoke after being nudged by her friend.

He shook his head.

"No?" Leah sounded surprised.

"Figured she's here to convince you to do the feature. I'm guessing she did if you're not running out of here to the airport." Wade leaned back in his chair, his hands wrapped around the warm mug in front of him. He probably should buy Betsy a box of Sage's best chocolates as a thank you.

Hell, he'd buy her a year's supply.

"About that..." Leah drawled out the words, leaning close, elbows on the table. "I kind of agreed to stay if the focus could be on Marietta. It's perfect timing with the scavenger hunt happening tomorrow, you know?"

He nodded. It made perfect sense to him. He'd basically said as much to her last night.

"But..." Betsy added.

Wade looked toward Betsy and caught the huge grin on her face, reminding him of a cat who'd just caught a fish and enjoyed every last bite of it, and then toward Leah who looked like she'd just swallowed a horse fly.

"But?" Wade prompted.

Leah opened her mouth, but no words came out.

"Let me guess. This is where that whole *Lonely Leah Finds Love* thing comes in right?" If it was, sign him up.

Leah nodded, her face turning an even brighter shade of red than before.

"How can I help?" he offered.

Betsy slapped the table with her hand. "See, told you he'd be up for it. And you were all worried..."

"Betsy," Leah said between tight lips.

"What? He said he'd help." She shrugged her shoulders before looking at her phone. "Oh, I need to answer this. Be right back." The phone was glued to her hear before she'd stepped away from the table. She headed outside and stood in front of the window, one arm holding the phone to her ear, the other wrapped around herself as if trying to remain warm.

"Maybe I should take her coat to her?" Leah offered.

Wade shook his head. "If Cali girl can't figure out it's still winter up here, she will soon enough." He took a look beneath the table and snickered at the rubber boots Leah still wore.

"You know you can get things shipped here within a day, right? Why don't you order yourself a good pair of boots? Especially if you're staying a while longer."

A smile bloomed on her face. "Done and done. Dylan suggested the same…" She immediately stopped and looked at him with wide eyes. "H-he suggested that last week and I…Betsy said the same thing a few minutes ago." She stumbled over her words, obviously caught in a lie.

Wade heard it. He also heard what she didn't say.

"So you're saying you already ordered some, is that it?" He studied her for the tells she gave when she lied.

"I did. Should be here tomorrow." She avoided looking at him, turning her gaze to the window and watching her friend freeze outside.

"About that offer to help, did you mean it?" she asked.

He waited for her to look at him before he answered.

"You know I did." He put all his heart into those words.

Leah straightened in her chair, her hands wrapped

around her mug, like his, and she looked anywhere and everywhere but at him.

Spit it out, was what he wanted to say to her.

"Will you pretend we're together? Like together-together?" She barely whispered her question.

"No." The word came out faster than he'd intended.

Hell no, he wasn't going to pretend. Having her ask him to hurt. More than he thought it would. He wasn't going to lie. For a moment, there had been hope that she'd stayed, not just because of Betsy but because of him, but…maybe he was wrong.

"No?" She looked at him then. This time, he was the one to glance away. He didn't want her to see how much her question had affected him. "I know…" She sighed. "I know it's asking a lot, but Betsy and her crew will only be in town for a few days, and—"

"How many days?" he interrupted her.

"Three at the most. Today, they'll scout areas. Tomorrow, they'll film. The following day will be any required retakes, and then they'll leave." Leah worried her lip and moved her cup in circles.

"So you're wanting me to pretend that we're together? That we're in a relationship, in love, and are preparing a future together?"

Leah nodded.

"Here in Marietta, right?" Wade wanted to be clear on what he was supposed to be *pretending*.

She nodded again.

Wade rubbed the back of his neck while taking his time thinking about what she was asking.

It wasn't pretending on his part. He loved her, wanted to be in a relationship with her, and wanted her to be here, in Marietta, with him forever.

He wasn't sure he could pretend knowing she didn't want the same thing.

Because she didn't, right?

Except, after his talk with Dylan, he thought she did. Dylan had said Wade had broken her heart. That she'd said she loved him; only, he hadn't heard her.

So what was up?

Did she love him or didn't she?

Was she here to stay or was she only here to do the feature on Marietta?

Was she playing him, hoping he would be a willing participant?

Why did women have to be so damn difficult to read?

"Will you, please?" Leah pleaded. The color of her eyes had lightened, and he could see she was really worried that he wouldn't agree.

He didn't like to see her worried. But he didn't like how he was feeling inside either.

Torn. Confused. Hurt.

"Do you love me, Leah?" He decided to ask outright. He needed to know. No more being patient, no more waiting for her to admit what he thought they both knew. No more trying to be patient and hoping… He needed to know.

"Wade…" Leah swallowed hard, licking her lips. "I-I" She struggled, really struggled to answer him.

That was all he needed to know. Everything inside of him died as he watched her try to respond. If there was a switch he could flip to turn off all his emotions, he would have done it right there and then.

"That's all I needed to know. Your brother is under the impression you told me you loved me and I didn't respond, except, we both know if you'd actually said those words, things would be a lot different now." He pushed his chair away with more strength than he'd intended.

"No, Leah. I can't pretend. I'm sorry. Maybe you were right last night, maybe things have changed between us and it's time I accept it." His chest squeezed, and there was no air left in his lungs for him to breathe. Everything hurt. If he didn't leave right now, he wasn't sure if he would survive.

He briefly closed his eyes, not wanting this moment to be the last one he remembered of her, and turned.

He heard Sage calling out to him, but he couldn't stop so he plowed right through the door, brushing past Betsy who stood there with her mouth gaped wide open, and headed for his truck.

His life was crashing down around him, and it was all because he couldn't keep his mouth shut.

Chapter Seventeen

L EAH COULDN'T MOVE. She was frozen in her chair, everything inside of her stiff and unrelenting.

She wanted to call out to Wade to stop, to stay, to listen to her.

Except, she couldn't. Her mouth was perma-frozen wide open, but no words would come. She wanted to throw up as she watched the man she loved walk away from her.

"What happened?" Betsy barged into the store looking bewildered. "Wade just ran past me, and he looked upset. I tried to stop him, but he didn't even hear me."

"He said no." Leah managed to get those words out. Her voice was a mere whisper, but it sounded like she'd shouted just to be heard over the sound of her breaking heart.

Betsy sank down in the chair, speechless.

"I never thought he'd say no." Leah swallowed hard, the words a jumble of dry kindling in her throat. She blindly reached for her cup of cocoa and took a sip.

"Well, that's a little unexpected." Betsy rubbed her forehead with the palm of her hand. "He'll change his mind."

Betsy sat up, her shoulder blades a straight line as she did so. "Whatever you said, just go apologize and all will be well." She glanced at her watch. "I can take the team to scout areas while you go fetch that hunk of a man of yours."

"He's not mine." Leah's chin dropped, and the weight of everything she'd lost threatened to cave her body inward. What had she done?

"You need to apologize." Sage was at her side, her face clouded by a fury of storm-like emotions.

Leah had the feeling that in Sage's mind, hurting Wade was the unforgivable sin.

"I don't know what you've done or what's happened between the two of you, but go make it right," Sage continued.

"I was trying," Leah admitted. There was a boulder that sat inside her chest, and it got heavier the longer she sat there. "Sage, I don't know what I did. I stayed..." She pinched the bridge of her nose with her fingers and grimaced. "I stayed here instead of leaving. I thought...I thought he'd understand what that meant." She entwined her fingers together and twisted them until the bones cracked and her fingers turned white. "He accused me of running away last night, and I told him I wasn't."

Sage pulled out the empty chair at the table with a heavy sigh. "Leah, did you tell him specifically you stayed for him? That you are here for him? That you love him?"

Leah shook her head. No, she hadn't said any of those words.

"Then maybe you should." Sage stood, one hand on the edge of the chair. "Maybe it's time one of you stopped being so stubborn and just admitted what's in your heart." She placed her hand on Leah's shoulder and gave a tender squeeze. "God knows one of you needs to step up to the plate."

Leah looked to her friend, who gave a slight dip of her head in agreement.

"Hang tight and I'll place two hot cocoas in travel cups for you. I'm sure Wade could use another one." Sage stepped away and briefly chatted with a customer in line.

"Okay." Betsy leaned forward and whispered conspiratorially. "So maybe my idea wasn't the right one and if I made things a little...messy, I'm sorry. We can fix this though, I know it."

"Messy?" Leah rolled her eyes as a wave of hysterical despair underlined with anger rose inside of her. "More like screwed this up. You know, it's time I stop listening to your suggestions. I should know better by now; I really should."

She had to fix this.

"What did Wade actually say?" Betsy asked, her cheeks a solid pink as she thankfully didn't even try to defend herself.

Leah thought back to his words, to the hurt she saw in his gaze.

"He asked me if I loved him." She wanted to cry. He asked her if she loved him and how did she respond? "I couldn't say anything. I wanted to." She lifted her gaze to look Betsy in the eyes. "I wanted to but…"

"You were too afraid," Betsy completed her sentence. "So go tell him. Tell him you love him. Tell him everything that's in your heart." She reached across the table for Leah's hands. "It's not too late."

Leah wanted to hope that. She really did. But she knew Wade. He would only take so much before he shut down. He was the first person to give someone a chance, even a second chance, but take advantage of him too often, hurt his heart one too many times…and he was done. He believed she didn't love him. Believed that this whole charade with *Charmed* and Betsy was exactly that—a charade.

Except it wasn't. She didn't want to pretend that they were in love.

She wanted to be in love.

She was in love.

"Then tell him that," Sage whispered in her ear as she set the cups of steaming cocoa down on the table. "Don't tell anyone else how you feel until you tell him. He deserves that much."

Leah looked up at her old friend. "I will." She licked her dry and chapped lips as she thought about where he could be right now.

Knowing Wade, he wouldn't have gone home. He would be out in the field, trekking through the snow and broken branches, trying to find some semblance of peace in his soul.

There was only one place he would go.

She glanced down at her rubber rain boots with dismay. "Betsy, I need your car keys, please." She held her hand out.

"But...all our equipment is in there. And we need to—" Betsy stopped at the glare from Sage. "We'll just walk around town to scout out areas," Betsy said instead of what she was going to complain about. "Maybe Sage can explain how the scavenger hunt works." She directed her remark to Sage as she pulled the keys out of her pocket and handed them to Leah.

"Once things calm down in here, sure, I can take a break and tell you about the coins and what we'll do." Sage stepped to the side so Leah could stand. "Go get him, honey, and don't come back until you've told him exactly how you feel."

Leah gave her a quick hug before she dashed out of the store and into the large SUV Betsy had rented, determined to do exactly that—find Wade and tell him how she felt.

HER FINGERS DANCED nervously along the steering wheel as she pulled up beside Wade's truck. She saw his footprints buried deep in the snow until they disappeared into the bush, and she groaned. She'd really been hoping he'd stayed in the truck, where it was warm.

After adjusting the scarf he'd made for her around her neck, Leah nudged the vehicle door with her hip and followed him, carrying the two cups of cocoa in her hands.

She tried to walk in his footsteps, but his stride was too

long and rather than fall face-first into the snow, she sucked it up and made her own path, her toes freezing thanks to the rubber boots. What happened to all the snow melting, huh Dylan? Her brother really needed to start forecasting properly.

Ten minutes later, she found him.

He leaned against a tree, arms crossed over his chest, his eyes sorrowful as he watched her come to him.

She stopped a few feet away and breathed in the crisp air, letting it inflate her lungs and praying that he wouldn't turn her away before she could share her heart.

"Sage sent me with this." The words came out before she could stop them. She held out the cup, but he didn't move.

"Is that the only reason you came out here in those go-dawful boots? Sure you can handle the cold and snow after living on the beach?" His voice, while soft, was edged like a sharp knife and cut deep.

She kicked her foot out in front of her. The boots weren't so bad. Sure, they were yellow and stood out like a sore thumb and they did nothing to keep her feet warm. In fact, it was like the snow packed onto the boot with each step she took until her feet felt like they were ensconced in an igloo, but...

"Maybe I should have bought bright yellow snow boots. They're kind of growing on me."

She caught the tilt of his full lips as he struggled not to smile.

That gave her hope.

"Wade," she breathed his name, her nerves all scattered, "I…" She couldn't clear her thoughts enough, not with him looking at her like that.

Like he didn't believe any good would come out of this conversation.

"Spit it out, Leah," he said. There was a twinge of tenderness in his voice…at least, she hoped there was.

She breathed in deep.

"I didn't like you leaving me like that." She spoke with complete honesty, realizing that he deserved nothing less.

"I needed time to think."

She swallowed hard. "I know. But…"

"But what?"

Leah pressed her fingers to her lips and pinched hard.

"But what, Leah?" Wade pushed himself away from the tree he'd leaned on and stood in front of her, his gaze steady.

She wanted to look away. Not because she was uncomfortable or what she had to say was anything but the truth, but because that was exactly what it was…the truth, and she was nervous about how he'd respond.

"You didn't give me enough time to respond to your question."

From the way his gaze melted as he watched her, she was very thankful she hadn't looked away.

He didn't say anything, just watched her. She grew warm beneath his gaze. Not toasty-warm-in-front-a-fire feeling, more like melting-from-his-smolder warm.

"Do you have any idea how long it took me to make this scarf?" He touched the wool around her neck, his fingers hooking through the holes, and then he pulled.

Only a few inches separated them now.

"Josie wouldn't let me give up. I begged her to knit it for me, but she wouldn't have it. Said it wouldn't mean the same. I remember your reaction when you unwrapped it…do you?"

Remember? Of course she did. A scarf full of holes was the last gift she'd expected, and she was sure it had showed on her face. But what did that have to do with this?

"That scarf has always reminded me of our relationship. It's not perfect and nowhere near what I thought it would be by now, but…" He ran his hand behind her head and threaded his fingers in her hair. "Every time I see you wear it, I think how perfectly it suits you. Like you suit me."

"I suit you?" A flurry of swallows took flight inside her skin, and every part of her danced in a distinct but harried rhythm. They'd never been this close before. Not on purpose. She didn't know where to look—his melt-worthy gorgeous blue eyes or his kiss-worthy amazing lips.

He pulled her closer.

She couldn't breathe.

"You suit me. You don't just make me a better person, you make me a different person. You make me want to be a better man—not just for you or for those around me, but for myself, too. You also exasperate me and drive me batty on the best of days, but I'd be disappointed if you didn't. I want you in my life, Leah. But not like this."

His warm breath brushed across her face, and she had a hard time concentrating on what he was saying to her.

"Not like this?" What was wrong with this? This seemed perfectly fine right now…especially if he kissed her. This would then be perfect.

"Not like this," he repeated himself with a hint of laughter in his voice, as if knowing exactly what he was doing to her. "Not only as friends. I need more. I want more. If that's too much for you…I won't stick around and wait. I can't. So I need you to decide."

Leah licked her lips, her gaze now completely on his mouth. She watched him form the words, heard what he'd said, but it took a moment to register.

"You need me to decide." She nodded her head and went to pull back slightly, as if to get her bearings, but his hold on her head wouldn't let her move. "That's why I'm here." She looked him in the eyes, full on, and her heart melted by the look of love in his own.

"You've made a decision?"

She nodded before releasing the full throttle of her love for him in her smile.

"I love you, Wade Burns. I've loved you for a long time, but I was too afraid to admit it. I tried to tell you how I felt before I went on the show, but I think…I don't think you heard me." She swallowed hard and forced the words to come out before she could stop herself. "I thought you didn't feel the same way anymore but didn't know how to tell me, and it broke my heart. Then Betsy convinced me to go on that stupid show, and I made a bloody fool of myself, which made me come here. But I didn't know how to face you after confessing how I felt and—"

"You were in the bath when you called me, weren't you?" His voice deepened, his eyes turned a husky blue, and his fingers rubbed the back of her neck with mesmerizing strokes.

She nodded, completely embarrassed that he'd known. It had been the first time she'd ever called him like that...

"Do you have any idea what that does to a man? To know you're talking to him, covered only with water and bubbles? I could barely concentrate on your words, Leah...and I had to hang up after I heard you move in the water. I could barely hear you, but the picture in my mind..."

"You couldn't hear me?"

She knew the moment he was talking about. She could see it so clearly in her head. She'd said *I love you* and sat up in the water at the same time, moving fast enough that the water had spilled over the edge of the tub. The sound had echoed in her very small bathroom.

She should have known he hadn't heard her.

"Tell me again," Wade said.

No. Not said. Demanded. In a I-need-to-hear-you-say-it-before-I-drown type of insistence.

"I love you," she whispered.

"I love you," she breathed.

"I love you." She loved—with all her heart, she loved those very words, as if they were chocolate for her soul. She loved him with everything inside of her and if he-didn't-kiss-her-this-very-instant-she-was-going-to-explode.

He closed the remaining distance between them. When he touched his lips to hers, she breathed out one final word that said everything she'd ever felt and would feel about this kiss.

"Finally."

Chapter Eighteen

L EAH SAT AT the small corner table in the Copper Mountain Chocolate Shop, a large mug of Sage's amazing cocoa and a small box of assorted chocolates in front of her. Her fingers were wrapped around the warm mug and she flashed a warm and truly heartfelt smile at Betsy, who sat slightly off to the left.

"How did I feel about the name Lonely Leah?" She repeated Betsy's question for the camera. "To be honest, it hurt. Sometimes, the truth hurts, right? But if it hadn't been for that name forcing me to run home to heal my broken heart, I probably wouldn't have built up the courage to tell Wade how I really feel about him." She glanced out the window to where Wade rested against his pickup truck. He gave her a wink before he turned to talk with her brother.

The sun was just about to go down as she completed what Betsy promised would be the last of the plethora of interview segments for the *Charmed* feature. Segments where her and Wade spoke as a couple, where it was just Wade, then her, and then little side ones with her brother, Grams, and even Sage.

Betsy made true on her promise. They shot these segments all over town and focused on Marietta and the people here that Leah loved with all her heart.

"I was looking for love when I came on *Charmed*; I just didn't realize that I was looking in the wrong place." She said this, not only for Betsy and to help her save face when it came to her job, but also for all those who would watch the show from here in Marietta, those who already knew that her and Wade were meant to be together.

The butterflies in her stomach wouldn't stop. She knew it had nothing to do with all the cocoa she'd been drinking today and everything to do with the man who stood outside the window.

The man who was hers.

After finding him out in the bush yesterday, after that life-changing kiss she'd finally experienced, her whole life changed.

At least, that was how it felt for her.

When she couldn't handle her frozen toes anymore, they returned to their vehicles and drove back to Dylan's house. They curled up on the couch, with Wade rubbing her feet as they talked about what this meant for them and their relationship.

Wade hadn't been kidding when he said he couldn't do this anymore.

He asked her to move back to Marietta full time, with

him.

First thing this morning, Leah had left a voice message for her boss, asking if they could discuss some changes. She wanted to move back here, she really did, but she didn't want to stop working for KIND. If she still had a job, she wanted to see how open they would be to her living in Montana while working for them.

She didn't want to return to California. Not now. Not ever, unless it was for a quick trip.

Betsy made a roll motion with her hand, indicating time to wrap up to the crew, and Leah breathed a sigh of relief.

"All done," Betsy said. "I don't think we need to redo anything, and that was just about perfect. A little bit of editing and it'll be a fairy tale come true for the little hick girl from Marietta. It's perfect."

"So no more?" Leah wanted to make sure.

"Nope, I don't think so. Why?"

Leah took a long gulp of her hot cocoa, not even noticing the scald down her throat, before she stood, leaned down to give her friend a kiss on the cheek, and shrugged her coat on.

"I have a hot date planned with that man outside, and I'm itching to get back out on the ice. I'd prefer to do it without a camera crew following me around."

"Oh, come on." Betsy stood with her. "It hasn't been all that bad, right?"

Leah glanced over at Sage who stood at the counter, a

slight frazzled look on her face. "I think Sage would like some breathing room in her shop," she said.

At least Betsy had the decency to look guilty. "I know, I'm so sorry." Betsy raised her voice. "I didn't think we'd take this long. I'll make it up to you," she said to Sage. "I promise."

Sage waved her away, as if it wasn't important, but Leah caught the flash of relief on her face.

"You'd better buy out her stock of boxed chocolates, at the very least," Leah prompted.

"Done and done. *Charmed* is also going to be paying her plenty for these hours of inconvenience." Betsy gathered her bag, stuffing all her notebooks and other things into it. "Just let me chat with the crew for a minute about the next steps, and I'll meet you outside."

Leah barely heard her. She was out the door so fast and at Wade's side before Betsy even realized she was gone, no doubt.

She shivered with a rush of anticipation and excitement when Wade placed his arm around her and pulled her close.

"Listen, if this is the way things are going to be, keep it at your place. Okay, buddy?" Dylan said as Leah leaned into Wade's embrace. She loved the way it felt to be held by him. He towered over her, for sure, but she felt sheltered, safe, and secure—more than she'd ever felt in her life.

This was where she belonged. In his arms. She couldn't believe it had taken her so long to realize it.

"That's what I'm trying to convince her of," Wade said as he placed a kiss on the top of her head.

"Whoa…" Leah looked up at him. "Let's not rush into things, okay? One step at a time." Although, truth be told, she was okay about rushing. It felt natural to take this next step in their relationship, and she was quite looking forward to it.

"On that note." Wade reached into his jacket pocket and pulled out a folded piece of paper. "This is for you."

The grin on his face reminded her of Dylan's cat, Jack, after catching a mouse in the basement.

"What's this?" She took the paper and opened it, squealing with delight at what she read.

"I figured now would be the perfect time to go on that trip of ours to Napa," Wade said.

She caught the wink between him and her brother and knew she was out of the loop on something important. She didn't care at the moment, though—she was headed to Napa Valley with Wade on a romantic weekend away.

She read the name of the hotel and couldn't believe Wade had booked it. She knew how much this hotel cost, knew because it was the one place in Napa she'd been wanting to visit but couldn't afford.

"Is this all from…" She looked up and caught the telltale smiles on both Wade and Dylan's face. "Wait a minute…" They didn't, right? They wouldn't…they couldn't…Dylan was horrible when it came to forecasting the weather, right?

"I don't know what you're about to accuse me of, but you'd better stop before you say anything else. I would never, in good conscious, do anything to hurt my career or the name of the radio station I work for. Not even if the whole town was involved and wanted to ensure Wade took you to the most romantic location you've ever dreamed about. Not even then. Got it?"

Leah blinked away the tears of extreme happiness she felt in this moment.

And to think she'd almost thrown it all away because she'd been too afraid.

The End

You'll love the next book in…

Love at the Chocolate Shop series

The rest of the Love at the Chocolate Shop is coming soon!
Available now at your favorite online retailer!

About the Author

Steena Holmes is the *New York Times* and *USA Today* bestselling author of the novels *Saving Abby, The Word Game, Stillwater Rising and The Memory Child,* among others. She won the National Indie Excellence Award in 2012 for *Finding Emma* as well as the USA Book News Award for *The Word Game in 2015.* Steena lives in Calgary, Alberta, and continues to write stories that touch every parent's heart. To find out more about her books and her love for traveling, you can visit her website at www.steenaholmes.com or follow her journeys over on Instagram @steenaholmes where she's always on the hunt to find the best chocolates around.

Thank you for reading

Charmed by Chocolate

If you enjoyed this book, you can find more from all our great authors at TulePublishing.com, or from your favorite online retailer.

TULE
PUBLISHING

Made in the USA
San Bernardino, CA
23 March 2017